© 2021 Cara Maxwell

All rights reserved. No part of this book may be reproduced, or stored in a retrieval system, or transmitted in any form or by any means, electronic, mechanical, photocopying, recording, or otherwise, without express written permission of the publisher.

For permissions contact:
caramaxwellromance@gmail.com

This is a work of fiction. Names, characters, places, and incidents either are the product of the author's imagination or are used fictitiously. Any resemblance to actual persons, living or dead, events, or locales is entirely coincidental.

Cover design by: B.K. Andrews

Cara Maxwell

Chapter 1

From what he could see of Paris, Christopher was less than impressed. In the distance, the buildings were slowly rising up from the morning fog. The smoke from early-lit fires spiraled from chimneys and mingled with the dewy mist. The Seine snaked like a serpent between the wide boulevards. Though he was too far away to see clearly, it was easy enough for him to imagine. The streets would be slowly filling with working-people off and about their business. These would mingle with revelers returning home, less than steady from their merriments.

It would no doubt be much the same as London or Edinburgh or Seville. Large cities were all the same, Christopher thought scornfully. What did people find so special about Paris?

"It is beautiful, no?" His companion mused, breaking into Christopher's solitary thoughts. Christopher made a noncommittal sound, hoping the other man wouldn't feel the need to expound further.

The chipper voice was like a hammer in his pounding head.

He drank too much last night, he admitted internally. The wise thing to do would have been to excuse himself to his room right after he had concluded his supper. He was traveling with a hired companion; he had no obligation to stay below and socialize. But when had Christopher been described as wise? No, instead he sat in the busy tavern, staring at the hodgepodge of travelers talking and carousing, trying to distract himself with pitcher after pitcher of strong ale.

"Ah, I can see my lady Notre-Dame. Isn't she something, monsieur? Surely you have nothing in England to compare." The young Frenchman continued eagerly, much to Christopher's chagrin. He was taking his duties as a guide into the city too earnestly. Christopher raised his eyebrows, but still said nothing. He didn't feel like arguing this morning. The pounding behind his eyes wouldn't permit it.

Despite himself, he did look closer, making out the twin towers of the cathedral's western façade. They rose far above the surrounding buildings, as if in physical declaration of the famed French building's supremacy and importance. It was indeed beautiful. But as they rode on, and the city drew slowly closer, Christopher could not see the beauty. Rather, his gaze seemed to blur, fuzzy at the edges, and it wasn't because of the ill-effects of drink.

He rubbed his hand over his face, as if he could rub away the memories. Through his entire journey to Paris, he had staunchly kept his mind focused on business. He planned for how he could make this foray into France profitable; thought strategically about what connections he might make that would further his business interests at home. He played many games of chess. He drank, a lot. Christopher had tried very hard to keep his memories of her at bay, even as he journeyed across a continent with the express purpose of searching for her. But Paris was in his sights now. Pragmatically, he knew that he couldn't hold back forever. He sighed deeply and let them come.

She flew across his mind in a tangled web of interconnected moments and memories. He could see her smiling conspiratorially. He could hear her laughing as she glanced over her shoulder, her long blonde hair caught in the wind. He could feel her lips, her breath skittering across his…

Damn! He gritted his teeth angrily. This was why he didn't think of her. It was far too easy to get swept back up into those old memories and feelings. That was *over*. She had made her choice, and he had made his.

Meera had chosen Paris. She had chosen it over familiarity, over security, over home. She had chosen it over him. And so, Christopher had banished her from his mind and he had avoided Paris at all costs.

There had been many instances where he might have visited the famous city. He had spent the last decade building up his personal mercantile investments. Many times, there were opportunities he could have furthered by traveling to Paris. But he sent others, or avoided them entirely in favor of other endeavors. Because Meera was in Paris. And while no one would call Christopher Bowden wise, most also wouldn't call him a fool.

Damn it, Christopher cursed again under his breath. *Damn the woman*. He had moved on; built a new life, new friends, new estate, new business. None of it was connected to Meera and that was exactly the way he wanted it. He did not want to remember the pain he felt when Meera left so unexpectedly for Paris. But then the damn woman had to go and disappear, surely getting herself into some interminable shenanigans. And her sister, Madison, recruited him to go and find her. *Damn Meera, damn Madison, damn it all*.

"Monsieur…" The other man inquired timidly, finally having surmised that the surly Englishman he was escorting did not want to hear any more about Paris.

Christopher shook himself free of the haze…from memory or drink, he wasn't sure…and answered, trying not to sound too irritable, "Yes, what is it?"

"We are nearing the city. We may enter through several routes; what is the direction of your accommodations?"

"It doesn't matter; I just need to get into the city." Christopher said shortly.

"I beg your pardon, Monsieur, but the city is quite large. I can help you find the most direct route…"

"That is not necessary." Christopher said brusquely. He dug into the pocket of his coat, withdrawing some of the money stowed there. He handed it to the young Frenchman, who looked confused. "Thank you for your help. This is the other half of your fee. I can find my own way from here."

The pair reigned their horses in to a slow walk while they spoke, but as soon as the guide accepted the money Christopher kicked his mount and started forward at a brisk canter. The younger man looked after him, bewildered at his unceremonious dismissal.

For a moment, Christopher almost felt bad for him. But he shook that off. He had been careful for the entire journey; keeping a guide only through two or three towns at a time, never mentioning his final destination, changing mounts often, keeping his mouth shut. He was relatively sure that he hadn't been followed. It was unlikely that whoever was responsible for Meera's disappearance had been diligent enough to read her sister's correspondence or keep close tabs on her aunt in Paris. But Christopher was thorough; it was what made him such a successful businessman. He had no idea what he was walking into here in Paris, but he would not be caught unawares. Not by Meera's captors or by Meera herself.

He recalled his last conversation with Madison before he left London. She snuck into his home, berating him mercilessly, and then demanding he make this ridiculous quest. Like an idiot he had agreed. Before she left him alone to his thoughts, she set a heavy packet of papers on his lap: her last few months' correspondence with Meera, and with her aunt since Meera's disappearance. She moved to leave but then turned back, her hand touching his shoulder so softly he wondered at first if he was imagining it. "She is not the same person she was, Christopher. And neither are you."

Madison's words echoed through his mind as the road beneath his horse's hooves turned from dirt to cobblestones. He was not the same lovestruck boy whom Meera had abandoned so abruptly. But it didn't matter to him who Meera was now. He was here to find her, to make a few profitable business advances, and then to leave. He would not let himself get pulled in again; he had been down that road before, and he had learned that lesson. Meera was in his past, and aside from this little blip, she would stay there.

Reigning in his horse, Christopher took a deep breath and looked down the Parisian street now fully illuminated by the risen sun and busy with foot and horse-traffic. "Ho there!" He caught the attention of a likely looking cart driver. "Can you direct me to the quartier Francois-Premier?"

Christopher listened carefully, and then without looking back rode directly into Paris.

Chapter 2

It did not take him long to find the home of Meera's great aunt. Located in an obviously well-to-do part of town, the streets here were considerably quieter. The who's who of French society were not early risers. The only people walking the streets were servants. Christopher was inconspicuously dressed, but he had an imposing bearing. As he dismounted his horse and rummaged in his saddlebag, passersby gave him a wide birth as they observed him curiously. No one was mistaking him for a servant.

He stood on the corner adjacent to the elegantly built French townhouse for almost a quarter of an hour, pondering his next move. Madison and Meera's elderly great aunt surely was not awake. It was no more than an hour past dawn. But if Meera was in danger, time was of the essence. Christopher couldn't afford to wait until what might be deemed a 'fashionable hour.'

Making up his mind, he crossed into the small courtyard that set the house back from the street, leading his horse by the bridle. At first, he thought he was alone; the place appeared deserted. But then a young groom appeared, rubbing his eyes, clearly regretting that he was no longer abed. Christopher suppressed a small smile; he could sympathize. There were places he would rather be himself.

"Bonjour Monsieur," the young man made a short bow, his blond head bobbing respectfully. "Are you expected this morning?" He asked, his tone dubious.

"I am here to speak with Lady Braxton. This is her home, yes?" He raised an eyebrow at the groom.

"Oui, Monsieur. But the lady does not usually accept callers at this hour." The groom took the bridle of Christopher's horse, but his voice and demeanor remained skeptical.

Christopher sighed with impatience. "I imagine not. However, no matter what abominable soiree she attended late into the night, she will have to be roused so I can speak with her."

"You misunderstand, Monsieur," the young man tried to say, but Christopher cut him off. This was not a promising start.

"Please inform the butler that I need to see Lady Braxton immediately. Then see that the horse is fed and watered. I will have need of him later today, and I want him ready to go." Christopher ordered. He turned dismissively, intending to enter the house. When he raised his eyes, they fell instead on an elegantly dressed woman atop a stunning dapple-gray steed.

Olivia Braxton appraised Christopher with a steely gaze. Although she was not young, it was impossible to gauge her age strictly from appearance. Her tightly bound hair was a mix of blonde and gray that looked like a jeweler had crafted a silver and gold alloy. She was dressed in a deep purple riding habit which she filled out well, and sat atop the horse with obvious comfort and grace. She dismounted without the help of the groom who had taken Christopher's horse, nor that of the soberly dressed man accompanying her.

"Who exactly are you, ordering around my staff before we've even had a spot of breakfast?" She asked, gray eyebrows arched. She handed her gloves to the man who had dismounted behind her, and set her hands firmly on her hips.

"Lord Bowden, my lady," He made a short bow, before raising his eyes to meet hers. "Madison sent me."

She stared at him inscrutably for a moment, and then nodded her head. "Henri? Please see the horses walked out and brushed down before they are stabled. We've had a brisk ride this morning." As soon as she started talking, the young tow-headed groom sprang into action. "Come, Lord Bowden, I am hungry."

Christopher followed her up the stairs and into the house. He did not have time for a full appreciation of his surroundings as he followed Lady Braxton through the foyer, past a few rooms, and into the dining room. But he saw enough to realize just the amount of wealth, and therefore importance, that Meera's aunt possessed. He was quickly revising his original image of her as an elderly spinster in desperate need of his help and attention.

A full breakfast had been laid on in the dining room. Lady Braxton took the seat at the head of the long mahogany table and motioned for Christopher to join her.

"Madam," Christopher nodded his head respectfully as he took the seat she indicated. He was beginning to get a sense of the woman. She was in charge and used to being so.

Lady Braxton rewarded him with an ironic smile. As if by silent summons, a footman appeared with a freshly brewed pot of tea and began to pour. Lady Braxton did not say anything until she had her cup in hand and had taken a long, slow drink. Then she cleared her throat and set down the steaming cup in its saucer.

"Well, Lord Bowden, I do apologize for my brusque manner. I am not used to receiving guests this early in the morning." She said.

"I understand completely, my lady." Christopher sipped his own tea slowly before continuing. He was an accomplished businessman, and the more he observed Lady Braxton, the more he began to see her as a tough potential business associate he needed to win over. And if he was going to find Meera, and get the hell out of Paris, he certainly needed Lady Braxton on his side. But it wasn't hard to understand her skepticism, given the circumstances.

"Quite honestly, I was surprised myself. It is a rare woman who is awake and in the saddle before dawn." He said smoothly. The corner of Lady Braxton's lips twitched into a small smile.

"A compliment or a commentary? I'm really not sure." She retorted. "Either way, a morning ride does wonders for the appetite. Let's tuck in, before it gets cold. I do hate to see food go to waste." Without further pretense, she began to fill her plate from the sideboard. Christopher followed suit.

After a few minutes, she spoke again. "It has been my habit to ride early in the morning since I first came to Paris. Meera often joins me," her voice faltered slightly at the mention of Meera, but she continued on without acknowledging the pause. "I have been loath to change any of my routines. I suppose I keep expecting to come down one morning and find her mounted and waiting for me. But it hasn't happened, and now you are here."

"Now I am here." Christopher repeated. Olivia was staring determinedly down at her plate, and Christopher noted the slight tremble in her hand. She covered her discomfiture well, quickly putting down her fork and readjusting her napkin in her lap. It was clear that she had a deep affection for her niece. He filed that information away, wondering if Meera reciprocated the emotion. The Meera he had known had given her affection freely and deeply. "Madison did not have much information to give me. Only a few letters she received from Meera and from you telling of her disappearance."

Appearing to have somewhat recovered, at the very least regained control of her emotions, Lady Braxton looked directly at him and nodded. "I didn't write to Madison as soon as Meera disappeared. I thought that maybe she had gone to stay with a friend, and her note letting me know had been misplaced. But after 2 days of no word and nothing turning up, I knew something was amiss. That is when I wrote to Madison, hoping against hope that perhaps Meera had gone there."

"It has been more than three weeks since she disappeared. Why have you not contacted the police?" Christopher tried to keep the sound of accusation out of his voice, but he saw Lady Braxton's lips tighten nonetheless. The question had plagued him from the first moment he took up this wild goose chase. When someone is missing, you go to the authorities. Unless you suspected they were caught up in something criminal. He suppressed a sigh; with Meera, nothing was outside of the realm of possibility. He carefully calmed his voice as he continued: "I apologize, I do not mean to asperse your judgement," he began, but Lady Braxton shook her head in negation.

"Meera is a very…" She paused, looking for the right word. "She is a very…eccentric young woman. While I trust her completely, I also cannot help but wonder if she may have gotten herself involved in something untoward."

"Untoward?" Christopher's eyebrows shot up.

"She would never do something illegal," Lady Braxton assured him. "But she does have quite the headstrong streak, and I was afraid that if I brought the officials into it she might not come out so favorably. She is an attractive, young, unmarried woman. My instinct is that she isn't injured or hurt, but the longer that she is gone, the more worried I am. She can be so reckless —"

Christopher couldn't contain the derisive scoff. Lady Braxton looked sharply at him. She leaned back in her chair and looked him over very carefully, making a thorough perusal of his features. Christopher didn't visibly squirm under her scrutiny, but he did begin to feel a little uneasy.

Finally, she asked: "What did you say your given name was, my lord?"

"I didn't," he cleared his throat. "My name is Christopher Bowden." He saw the flicker of recognition in the lady's eyes, and groaned internally. Maybe she wouldn't press him further.

No such luck. Olivia took a sip of her tea before asking delicately: "So you are already acquainted with Meera, then?"

This time Christopher sighed out loud. "More than acquainted." He said tersely.

The elderly but clearly spirited woman looked like she wanted to say more, but thankfully made the decision not to. Christopher breathed a silent breath of relief. He did not want to go into this territory at all. This was why he had not wanted to come to Paris for all of these years. For what seemed the hundredth time today, he silently cursed Madison and Meera for entangling him in this melee.

"I last saw Meera 23 days ago. She had been acting strangely for a few days, hastily leaving meals and making various excuses for not attending several of the social engagements we had responded to. I did not think much of it; when she gets a bee in her bonnet, there is no telling what she will do." She looked at Christopher as if waiting for a response. He carefully kept his face blank. She continued:

"On the day she disappeared, we took our customary morning ride. She insisted on a fast pace, and we were not able to speak much. When we returned, she said she was not hungry and excused herself. I did not see her again, but my butler informed me that she left just before midday to do some shopping. That is all I know."

Christopher had been nodding along, triangulating this new information with what he already knew about Meera's habits from having read her correspondence with her sister. "Did she go shopping alone?" He asked.

"Yes. That is not unusual. She sometimes meets friends, but often likes to accomplish tasks on her own. One of my footmen accompanied her." Olivia explained.

"I will need to speak with the footman immediately." Christopher was already beginning to get to his feet. "Thank you for breakfast, Lady Braxton. I will let you know when I have found any new information."

"I expect so," Lady Olivia nodded. She did not get up from her seat, but as he moved to exit the room, her words held him in place. "Meera may be impetuous and determined, Lord Bowden, but she is not foolish."

"I suppose that depends on your definition of the word." Christopher said archly. The lady met his eyes knowingly. She seemed to see right through him and it made Christopher distinctly uncomfortable.

Without shifting her gaze, she added: "It is reasonable to be cautious; time can alter people in unexpected ways. But it would be unwise to assume that you are the only one that carries the scars of the past. And the regrets of the road not travelled."

Chapter 3

It did not take long to locate the footman in question: a middle-aged Frenchman named Maximus who had been in Lady Braxton's employ for four years. He was a completely ordinary fellow with dark hair, slight build, and middling height. Perfectly deferential; Christopher could easily picture Meera walking all over him.

Lady Braxton insisted that they use her carriage to convey them to Paris' shopping district, in particular the Passage de Panoramas. Apparently Meera frequented the popular shopping street, with its brightly lit, ultra-modern gas lights and covered concourse. Christopher rolled his eyes; of course, Meera would be attracted to anything sparkly and new.

While he would have preferred to travel on horseback, rather than waste time as the carriage weaved and slowly navigated Paris' busy streets, it did mean that he had time to thoroughly question the footman.

"Tell it to me again," Christopher commanded, closing his eyes so he could concentrate. This would be the third time he asked Maximus to recount the story, and even with his eyes closed Christopher could sense the other man's growing exasperation.

"Miss Hutton wished to visit the paper shop, Susse, to replenish her supply of stationary. We took the Madame's carriage. Miss Hutton rode inside. I sat above with the driver. When we arrived, I assisted Miss Hutton down from the carriage. I told her it would only be a moment while I gave directions to the driver. She said she would go on ahead and I was to rejoin her when I finished."

"Why didn't she wait for you?" Christopher interrupted.

"I do not know, Monsieur."

"Did you accompany her on such outings often? Was she often so impatient?" He pressed.

The other man nodded and then shook his head. Noticing the perplexity, he clarified: "I have frequently accompanied Miss Hutton to le Passage. Many of her favorite shops are located here. But I would not describe Miss Hutton as impatient," Maximus said loyally. "It looked like it might rain; perhaps she did not want to get wet."

"Meera isn't afraid of the rain." He said without thinking. A brief image flashed in Christopher's mind: long blonde hair, curling into waves as the rain turned from a drizzle to a downpour. Instead of running for cover, the girl spun in a circle, almost dancing, dark eyes sparkling with laughter as she grabbed his hand and pulled him against her. Her body was unexpectedly warm amid the cool, damp air. With not inconsiderable effort, Christopher pulled himself back to the present.

He steeled himself against the memory, pushing it back down where it belonged. But despite his efforts, Olivia Braxton's voice floated into his head: *you are not the only one who carries the scars of the past.* Scars they were, there was no doubt about that.

"What happened next?" Christopher heard himself ask.

Maximus' face was blank. "Nothing," he said. "When I entered le Passage, I did not see her. I continued to Susse, but they had not seen Miss Hutton. When I could not find her, I returned home, thinking perhaps she had been unwell and taken another way home."

Christopher mulled on that for a few minutes. It could not have been far, from the carriage to the entrance of the shopping boulevard, and then to the paper shop, Meera's professed destination. Could someone have taken her in such a short time? In such a public place?

The carriage jolted to a halt, indicating they had arrived at their destination. As Christopher alighted from the carriage, he took careful note of the surroundings. They were on the Boulevard Montmartre. Two tall, proud stone columns announced the entrance to the row of shops. The weather was clear and several well-dressed patrons loitered outside of the entryway, casually conversing.

Christopher walked deliberately but not so slowly as to draw attention to himself. He might have been any gentleman inhabitant of Paris, strolling in to do his shopping. Maximus trailed behind him, pointing out where the carriage had stopped on that afternoon three weeks ago and blathering on about where the paper shop was located.

Feeling his annoyance beginning to rise, Christopher dismissed the footman to wait with the carriage. At first it looked like Maximus might protest, but then he seemed to think better of it, perhaps remembering his precarious position as the footman who had lost the Madame's beloved niece. Or maybe he had heard from his counterparts in the stable about Christopher's surly behavior. Either way, he retreated back outside without further protest. Christopher doubted the man had anything else of value to share, and he would just as soon be able to move about unencumbered.

As he moved down the street, he tried to take notice of anything that might be relevant. The glass overhead let in a considerable amount of light, and whatever gloominess might persist was augmented by the brightly lit gas lamps overhead. The shops themselves were colorfully arrayed, their windows artfully adorned and the doorways bustling with customers. It was busy; there were a lot of people moving about, and he could easily picture how Maximus could have lost sight of Meera quickly.

His first stop was Susse, home of fine writing materials that upper-class men and women required to keep up their correspondence. As he briefly surveyed the shop, he could not help appreciating the quality of the paper he rubbed between his fingers. He was, he reminded himself, part of this group. While he often forgot it, entrenched as he was in his business dealings and intent on making his own way in the world, he was nonetheless the younger brother of a viscount.

And it was that elite charm which he summoned as he approached the dark-haired woman behind the shop's high countertop. "Bonjour," she said politely, bobbing a faint curtsey.

"Mademoiselle," he smiled very intentionally; wide enough to look approachable, open, kind. Reserved enough to look mysterious, clever. He might be a natural charmer of women, but he had refined the skills considerably in his bachelorhood. The woman's eyes softened as she ran them over him. "Your establishment is quite lovely. I was just admiring your offerings." He nodded over his shoulder at the displays of papers, bound notebooks, and writing implements.

"You are too gracious," she batted her eyelashes, swaying her hips ever so slightly. She was an attractive woman and clearly knew it. Christopher felt a warmth kindling within him; she was just the sort of woman who would have held his fancy if he hadn't been there on other business. He reminded himself he had a purpose; it was easy when playing this game to get tangled up yourself.

"I am recently come from England, a friend of mine there recommended your shop."

"Oui? How kind of him…or her?"

Christopher chuckled. The woman wasn't exactly subtle. That's well enough, he thought. She was more likely to answer his questions. "A childhood acquaintance, Miss Meera Hutton?"

The shopkeeper's eyes widened a bit at that and she looked noticeably disappointed. That was interesting information, Christopher thought. Clearly, this woman perceived Meera to be enough of a prize that he would be unlikely to stray from her. Women were rarely wrong in these judgements, he had found. What was Meera like now?

Pushing that thought down, he leaned casually against the counter and deepened his smile. "We haven't seen one another in years, actually." The woman perked up noticeably. "When I said I would be travelling to Paris, she recommended several shops here in le Passage, but this was the only one I recalled. Perhaps you could help me," he paused here for effect, "Do you know what other shops she frequents?"

"Of course, monsieur, I am most happy to help. Miss Hutton is a gracious young woman and visits often." She gestured away from the counter, towards a cozy looking corner of the shop with a cushioned seat. "Perhaps I may show you some of our finer products, suitable to a gentleman of your taste, while we discuss?"

Half an hour later, Christopher exited the shop with a small parcel of stationary tucked under his arm and a mental list of six other nearby shops that Meera regularly patronized. He also had the shop woman's name, Arielle, and a thinly veiled invitation to return and get better acquainted. *Unlikely*, he sighed to himself.

He spent the next hour perusing shops and talking up shopkeepers, to little avail. All had been effusive in their praise: Meera was a loyal customer, a pleasure to talk to, a kind and interesting young woman. But none had seen her for several weeks, which a few noted was unusual. And none had seen her on the day in question.

It seemed impossible that Meera could have been taken against her will here amongst the shops. There were other shoppers everywhere, and no alleyways in which to secret her away without causing a commotion. Was it possible she had never entered le Passage de Panoramas at all? She could have made off down the street or around the corner while the footman's back was turned but…that implied she must have taken off on her own. That seemed even more ludicrous. What possible reason could she have for disappearing without a word? He dismissed the thought as unlikely; there had to be some other explanation.

His last stop was the milliner. He wasn't sure what his excuse was going to be for going into this shop; he certainly had no need for a lady's hat, nor anyone to purchase one for. Perhaps it was time for a more direct approach.

When he entered the store, he was greeted by a very young woman, perhaps only 14 or 15 years old. She looked vaguely alarmed at his presence, glancing apprehensively over her shoulder.

"Bonjour, Mademoiselle," He bowed slightly, thinking that she reminded him very much of his niece, who was 13 years old and quite skittish around strangers. The girl nearly toppled over the stand of hats she had been adjusting. Christopher caught it, righting it deftly.

"My father will be along shortly, Monsieur, to help you…" She managed to say, her voice trembling. Christopher smiled inwardly, clearly, she hadn't been expected a large, imposing, foreign male customer while her father was away. He took a step back from her to try and make her more comfortable.

"I am looking for my friend." He said plainly.

The girl looked surprised. "Please, let me summon my father,"

"Do you know Miss Meera Hutton? She is missing."

"Miss Hutton?" The girl stepped backwards, her brow furrowing. She leaned against the counter. "She has not been in for weeks, we have a commission ready for her. It is most unusual, she should have been to pick it up Thursday last. She has never been late to pick up an order. Of course, we might have delivered it, but she always insists on coming herself," She rambled on, seeming to forget that Christopher was there. But her head snapped up. "You're looking for her?"

"She is a friend," he said gently, careful not to scare the jumpy girl. "I have known her since we were children in England."

The girl nodded, still looking apprehensive but no longer like she was going to run away.

"When was the last time you saw Miss Hutton?" He asked.

"Last month. She came in to make a special order. She was planning to attend a masquerade ball, and wanted a special hat made." She paused, and Christopher started to ask a follow up question, but then stopped when the girl started to speak abruptly. "No – that was not the last time. Three weeks ago, or so, she came into the shop. I remember because we were very busy…I said hello to her, but I was with another customer. She walked to the back of the shop, but when I turned to help her, she wasn't there any longer." As she had spoken, the girl had turned towards the back of the shop, where a door stood partially ajar. She frowned.

"May I?" He asked, but didn't look back to see her awkward nod as he proceeded through the door. There were stairs leading up to a loft, a storeroom with various boxes and supplies, and a work station tucked into the corner. But there was another door. And that door opened onto an alleyway.

Chapter 4

"I stopped at this tavern here to have a pint and some victuals. Then I went to the warehouse, just there, to pick up my father's order. When I lifted up the blanket, there was nothing in the wagon. I loaded the crates and then went back to the shop." The young man explained. Christopher nodded but did not say anything. He surveyed the tavern and warehouse the boy, who was not much older than his sister, had indicated. Then he thanked the young man, gave him a few coins for his trouble, and sent him on his way.

Now Christopher stood alone, across the street from a reputable looking warehouse and a less than reputable looking tavern in Paris' bustling textile district. He quickly reviewed what he knew. On the day Meera had disappeared, the milliner's daughter had seen her briefly near the back of the shop. Later that day, the milliner's son had taken a wagon to pick up an order of ribbons and trimmings that his father had ordered from a merchant here in the textile district. When he went to load the wagon, it had been empty.

If Meera had been secreted away inside the wagon, huddled under a blanket, then she had departed sometime between when the young man arrived at the tavern and when he went to the warehouse. The idea of Meera huddled in a wagon, beneath a dirty canvas sheet, seemed preposterous. But it was his best theory so far.

She had not made it to the warehouse, so the tavern was his best bet. Christopher went inside, ordered a pint, and leaned against the bar to try and get the lay of the land. A busy taproom, serving mostly warehouse workers. Doorway near the back, perhaps to a private parlor for more genteel patrons. Stairs leading up in the back corner; most likely rooms for rent. He melted into the background as best he could, and when a couple of gruff looking men started the beginnings of a brawl, he slipped up the stairs. There were four doors. One was ajar; he looked inside but it appeared unoccupied. He stopped to listen at each of the other doors, trying to discern if there were voices or activity inside. He heard something clang to the floor in the furthest room.

Christopher tried to move as quietly as he could, but the floorboards gave a loud squeak. It would be obvious to whoever was within that there was someone on the landing. He gritted his teeth, and as fast as he could jimmied the simple lock with the small knife he kept in his boot, and swung the door open. He didn't hear the sound of his own body hitting the floor.

As the world around him blurred into focus, Christopher tried to ascertain how long he had been out. He had been in his fair share of fights and rough-and-tumble accidents growing up; this definitely wasn't his first time being rendered unconscious. He didn't think he had been under for more than a few moments; he felt groggy but not completely disoriented, and he could remember exactly what happened. Taking stock of the fact that he was not restrained in any way, he widened his gaze to take in the room, which was sparsely furnished. Perched on the edge of a large chest, arms and legs crossed, face inscrutable, was Meera.

"Was that really necessary?" He said, slowly raising himself up to sit.

"Well, I thought you meant me harm." She quipped.

"And a candlestick was how you chose to defend yourself?" He continued to take in his surroundings. The aforementioned weapon was on the floor near Meera's feet.

"It seems like it was effective to me." Meera uncrossed her legs but kept her arms tight around her in a clearly defensive stance. Christopher regarded her carefully. He could not help but notice how beautiful she was. She had lost the youthfully angelic glow he had known before and taken on a mature beauty. But the stubborn set of her mouth and the furrow of her brow had not changed at all. She was clearly not happy to see him. And that thought brought him back to reality; she might look a little different, but she was the same person. He could not allow himself to be haunted by old feelings now; he did not want or need that from her.

Meera had no idea what to think. A million thoughts were racing through her head and yet her mind was also strangely blank. He cleared his throat and pushed himself to his feet, suddenly looming above her. Her first coherent thought was that the Christopher standing before her was not the boy she had left in England a decade ago. This was a strong and virile man in his prime.

Christopher strode to the window, briefly glancing outside. It was clear that Meera had been occupying the room for some time; her personal items were carefully arranged on the small table beside the bed and her clothes were draped with care over the backs of two wooden chairs. Hell, even the bed was neatly made. The door locked from the inside. "So, you did run away of your own accord. Not the most gracious way to thank an aunt who clearly adores you." He said with a sigh.

Meera glared at him. "You do not know what you are talking about." When he rolled his eyes, she felt the intimidation he had initially inspired start to thaw, replaced with a growing burn. "The whole reason I came here was so that I could keep my aunt out of this matter."

"And what is this, Meera?" Christopher gestured around the room. "You shake off your footman, slip through the back door of your milliner's shop, hitch a ride to a disreputable part of town, and take up residence in a tavern? I knew you were careless, but even this seems like a stretch for you."

The burning in Meera's gut flared. No, this wasn't the Christopher she had loved all those years ago. This was a totally different man; harsh and bitter. Well, she wasn't the same person anymore either. She had never been one to bow to authority, and ten years of independence in a foreign country had only made her more firmly convinced of her own self-efficacy. "It is none of your concern, Christopher. I don't even know why you are here."

Christopher chuckled, but it was a humorless sound. "I am here because your aunt wrote to Madison when you disappeared without a word. And of course, Madison drafted me to come and find you."

This time Meera sighed. A shadow crossed her face; Christopher thought it might have been guilt. He felt a twinge of regret, even though it was exactly what he had been aiming for. Damn, she was slicing right through his defenses without even trying.

"Madison always was the worrier. Well, now you can report back that I am fine." Unsure what to do or say next, Meera leaned down and picked up the candlestick she had dropped on the floor, replacing it on the little bedside table. She thought she had planned everything out so nicely, but clearly something had gone amiss. Christopher was here, in Paris. There was no one in the world she could have less expected to walk through her door, tonight or any night. "Didn't Aunt Olivia receive my message?" She asked.

Christopher frowned. "There was no message."

Meera nodded, understanding at once. "I suppose that accounts for her concern. The little ruffian who I paid to deliver my note clearly didn't think it worth the time to travel uptown, once he had my coin in hand."

"Clearly." Christopher resisted the urge to chastise her further, but just barely. "Now let's go. It is late to be on the streets, but as long as I am with you we should be safe enough."

"I am not going anywhere." Meera said sharply.

"Did you not hear everything I just said? Your aunt and sister have no idea that you are even alive, for God's sake. Get your things together, and let's go." He repeated, his irritation evident in the clip of his voice even to someone who didn't know him as well as Meera did. Or had. Annoyed at his attempts to boss her around, she unconsciously re-crossed her arms and legs. He may be handsome as a god, but he was not going to tell her what to do.

"I understand that there has been some miscommunication, and I am sorry for it. I am sorry that you came all the way from England. But I have a mission here and I cannot just leave."

"A mission?" Christopher repeated blankly. He stared in disbelief at her slightly pursed lips: full, dark rosy pink, eerily familiar. Her crossed arms and legs did not hide the body beneath. In fact, clothed in only a nightgown, the curves of her body were barely covered. He determinedly fought back the ache of desire he felt building inside of him. "Enough of this, Meera. It is late."

Meera almost stamped her foot in frustration, but managed to quell the childlike urge. "You are free to go, Christopher. But this is too important for me to just abandon. I am in the middle of something here and I need to see it through. I know it's difficult to get anything through that thick skull of yours, but – "

"Be quiet."

"No, I will not be quiet, I – "

"*Meera, stop talking!*" Christopher whispered urgently. Taken aback by the tone in his voice, Meera stopped instantly. Christopher nudged her over towards the window, and took a slow, silent step closer to the door. He wasn't sure…but then there it was again. There was someone on the landing.

Spinning around quickly, Christopher grabbed her heavy fur pelisse from the back of the chair where it was draped and tossed it to her. "Put this on and get the window open," he ordered in a whisper.

Why was he so worked up? Meera glanced at the closed and bolted door that opened to the hallway. It did sound as if someone might be outside, but what of it? There were other rooms off the landing, nothing inherently suspicious about someone coming or going. He shot her a serious look over his shoulder. Shaking her head, she put her arms through the fur-lined sleeves and unfastened the window.

Meanwhile, Christopher lifted the trunk where she had perched earlier and positioned it in front of the door. He was quickly piling on top of it both the wooden chairs, tossing aside her neatly folded dresses carelessly.

"Really, Christopher, you are being ridiculous –" but she was cut off abruptly as someone began pounding on the door. Startled, Meera stumbled backward. Christopher caught her by the arm and pulled her towards the window. The intruder tried the door handle, and finding it locked, started pounding harder, clearly trying to force the door open.

Christopher did not waste a moment. He wrenched open the window and helped Meera onto the ledge. She looked down dubiously. "You cannot be serious."

He glanced around her. "Scoot along the ledge until you reach the side there, and then slide down to the edge of the roof and jump to the ground. It only looks like eight feet or so."

"*Only* eight feet or so?" Meera shot back.

"I thought you were fearless?"

"Fearless is not the same thing as stupid." She bit back, but she was already beginning to climb out the window per his directions. Christopher climbed up behind her as the door finally gave way.

A huge, roughly dressed man was visible through the makeshift barrier of furniture. That was all the motivation Meera needed to pick up the pace. She moved as quickly as she could, trying to ignore the clatter and shift of the shingles beneath her feet and hands as she made her way to the edge of the roof. There was a loud crash from inside the room, and then the large villain was leaning out the window. She glanced back long enough to get a clear look at his face: thick dark red hair, and a long scar running from the left temple down to the corner of his mouth. She shuddered, and then jumped.

Christopher hit the ground a second behind her. Not even taking the time to check for injuries, he grabbed Meera and hauled her around the corner of the tavern and out of sight of the window and the intruder. The street was mostly empty; a few people filtered in and out of the taverns intermixed with empty warehouses. Making quick decisions, Christopher took deliberate turns based on his limited knowledge of this area of Paris – really, just what he had observed while walking with the milliner's son – until they were suddenly on a much more populated thoroughfare.

"Where are we going?" Meera asked, lengthening her stride to match his. She did not know this area well, but Christopher was clearly walking with purpose. He did not respond, but kept doggedly on as if he did not hear her. "Where are we going?" She repeated.

"Meera, just be quiet and let me think!" He snapped.

Chapter 5

She wasn't sure what he was so upset about. They were both unscathed, if a bit breathless. And more importantly, she had a new lead. While she had no idea the identity of their attacker, there couldn't be that many red-haired giants with such distinctive scars frequenting the Paris textile district. However, a quick glance at Christopher's face advised her that she would do better not to mention her thoughts right that moment.

Christopher was desperately trying to keep his temper under control as he navigated the deserted back alleys of Paris. Unfamiliar with the city as he was, he did not know exactly where they were. But he knew the general direction of Lady Braxton's townhouse, and thereby a much safer part of town.

He was shocked that Meera didn't continue to pepper him with questions. He could not recall a single instance in their long history when Meera had done exactly as he asked.

As the streets became more brightly lit, the avenues widened and gave way to middle and then upper-class homes. Christopher felt some of the tension begin to release.

Meera's hand fit perfectly in his, he thought to himself. Wait...*what?* Had he been holding her hand the entire time? He must have grabbed it to ensure she didn't wander off; an entirely reflexive and reasonable action, he assured himself.

Her palm was soft and warm in his. Gradually he became aware of the weight of her body as she walked along behind him, having to make a slight effort to keep up with his wide stride. But she did not complain or even pant for breath. Whatever her life was like now, she clearly maintained her youthful exuberance.

Christopher dropped her hand abruptly. He did not care about her life now, he reminded himself. Meera tucked her hand into the pocket of her fur-lined pelisse, appearing completed unaffected.

They continued in silence for several more blocks before Christopher slowed and then stopped on a quiet street corner, poised on the edge of a thickly forested park. Meera looked up at him questioningly. While the area looked vaguely familiar, he was going to have to ask for her help.

"You know where we are, I trust?" He asked, eyebrows raised in expectation.

Understanding dawned in Meera's eyes, and he could have sworn he saw them start to twinkle just a little bit brighter. "Of course," she smiled. "I am glad we do not have far to go, my shoes were hardly made for this kind of a traipse across town."

"Indeed," Christopher said back. He crossed his arms, trying to look imposing. Meera smiled sweetly up at him. "Are you really going to make me ask?"

"Well, you have enjoyed bossing me around so much. It only seems fair that you should have to grovel a little." She crossed her arms in a mirror of his own posture, and in doing so made him feel ridiculous.

"It was my 'bossing you around' that saved our lives back there, Meera." Christopher said seriously, his voice a hard edge.

"I did well enough with my candlestick to put you down. I would have managed alright until I could have called for help." She protested, unconsciously pursing her lips in a stubborn pout. The expression was so familiar, and yet so startling, that Christopher almost didn't get his next words out.

"Maybe you could have taken out one. But that man was not alone; there were at least two behind him that I saw through the doorway, covering his rear. Your candlestick wouldn't have been much good then. No, they would have you. In whatever way they wanted."

His words hit Meera like ice. She may have her fair share of bravado, but she wasn't stupid. She swallowed hard and bit her lip. A sudden wave of emotion washed over her, and she dug her teeth hard into her lower lip to keep from dissolving into a pile of tears. *No*, she told herself. *Not now, not in front of him, not at all.*

Christopher immediately regretted the harshness of his words. Meera paled instantly. He could see the tremor that rippled through her body and the glistening in her eyes. But she did not cry, and she did not break down. She had certainly gained a better control of her emotions since he last knew her. She took a couple of deep breaths to steady herself, and then reached for his arm.

"Thank you," She said simply, squeezing his arm tightly.

This time, the current between them was electric. Christopher felt every long, delicate finger where it squeezed onto his arm. Gentle, but strong. It was as if his thick coat was not there at all. *What if it was not there?* The tantalizing thought of her skin on his sent a jolt through him.

Meera held onto his arm for so long because she was afraid that if she let go, she might fall over. She hadn't thought consciously about it at all; she was thankful to him, and it was a completely natural and innocent gesture. But it didn't feel innocent now.

He was so warm, she could feel it through the material of his coat. He had always been like that, seeming to generate endless heat somehow from within. How many times had she held herself close to him and soaked up that very warmth? Would it feel the same now? She wondered. Would it feel just as soothing, and yet exciting, as it had before?

There was a rustling in the bushes several yards down the path. They jumped apart like the touch had burned them. Scalded their souls, heated their memories. A small bird emerged, hopping excitedly on the cobblestones and letting out a few experimental chirps. The first caller of the morn.

"We should get going," Christopher said. "Lead the way." It was a directive, but this time it didn't feel like he was bossing her around.

She gave him a small smile, all she could manage as her emotions went topsy-turvy inside of her. "Of course," she said, and started to lead him across the street.

The first rays of the sunrise were just beginning to peak over the Paris skyline as Christopher and Meera entered the cobbled courtyard of her aunt's home. The gate was unlocked, which was unusual. Meera frowned slightly as Christopher moved aside the heavy wrought iron and ushered her inside. Suddenly, the large front door of the house opened.

Lady Braxton appeared in the doorway, silhouetted by the fully-alight house behind. Clearly, no one had slept the night in this household, Christopher observed. At first the older woman looked at him, seeking answers, but then her eyes lit on Meera. In what seemed no more than a blink, they were in each other's arms. Olivia mumbled something into Meera's hair as she held her tightly against her, and Meera's shoulders shook with laughter.

Christopher found himself smiling, but he couldn't help feeling like an interloper. Around the courtyard, Lady Braxton's staff were beginning to materialize. Christopher caught sight of the young groom he had met that morning. "Please have my horse saddled, I will be leaving as soon as you can make ready."

Catching his voice, the two previously incoherent women turned immediately to him. "Lady Braxton, I think it would be redundant to say, but I have found your niece." He said, bowing gallantly. Meera rolled her eyes, but Olivia just smiled.

"Indeed, you have." She said, her hand grasping Meera's firmly. "And so quickly too. When Maximus reported that you did not return from Le Passage, I hoped it meant you had a lead. I could not sleep, for waiting." She explained.

Before he could respond, she motioned for the blonde groom to halt. "Please, Lord Bowden. I desperately want to hear more details about what has occurred tonight, but looking at the two of you, I think some sleep is in order first. Meera, all of your things are just as you left them. I am sure the maids are upstairs turning down your bed and laying out your nightgown as we speak."

Meera sighed eagerly. She could not wait to slip into the clean, silky sheets of her own bed after so many nights spent in a tavern.

"Lord Bowden, I have had my staff prepare a room for you as well. Not knowing when you would return, it seemed prudent." Lady Braxton added.

"I appreciate it, my lady, but I have taken lodgings not far from here…" he began, but Olivia waved her hand in dismissal.

"That is no problem. Give the name of the hotel to my butler, and he will see that your things are brought over. Really, it is the least that I can do after you have returned Meera. I do not believe that any accommodations you have will meet the comfort of room and board you will find here." She assured him.

Christopher had the distinct feeling that he was being meddled with. He glanced at Meera. She raised her eyebrows, shook her head slightly, and gave the barest shrug of her shoulders. She did not know what her aunt was up to either.

"Alright…" He said slowly. "I will stay, so that I can be assured there is no further danger before I take my leave of Paris."

"Lovely," Olivia turned to the butler, poised at the doorway, and issued a few quick orders. "Sleep well, then, Lord Bowden," she said in farewell, turning and ushering Meera into the house before the young woman could add a word of her own.

Christopher stared at the doorway momentarily. *Damn if it isn't something in the blood,* he thought to himself as he stared after the two women.

Chapter 6

Meera slept right through breakfast the next morning. She was usually an early riser, but an exception could be allowed after a night like that. When she did wake, in her own bed, her first thought was how thankful she was for her aunt's luxurious taste in bed linens. Her second was of Christopher.

She shivered involuntarily. A shiver of anticipation or foreboding? She wasn't sure. The man she met last night might technically be the same person she had known and loved, but the man was completely different than the boy. The sweet, affable, funny, blonde-haired boy of her past seemed totally divorced from the sarcastic, bitter Adonis of the present. His bright blue eyes, always his most striking feature, had looked her over with sharp intelligence. His golden hair was cut and styled differently. He perfectly achieved to look of desirable rogue bachelor.

She knew virtually nothing about his life over the past ten years. When she first left England it had been so painful. She had carefully avoided mention of him in her correspondence with her parents and sister, and they had respected that silence. When her parents visited her two years later, her mother tentatively brought up Christopher's name. But Meera shut her down, and since then there had been no discussion. Madison mentioned him sometimes in her letters; enough that it was obvious he was still an active part of her sister's life. But Meera did not ask any further questions.

A handful of references in letters over the span of a decade should have been hard to conjure up. Meera was annoyed at herself by how easily she was able to recall the few details she did know. Apparently, she was not as emotionally removed from that aspect of her past as she liked to believe. Well, the burning she had felt last night when they touched was enough to confirm that.

What did she know about Christopher, this Christopher? He spent a fair amount of time in London and was a frequent guest at social gatherings held by her elder sisters, Madison and Leonora. Madison mentioned him returning from various trips and often referred to his business – whatever that business was? She didn't know. He was not married – that she did know. It was not much to go on. And that reminded her of her current predicament.

Meera was thankful to be alive, and whatever the complications that arose because of Christopher being here, she owed him a debt of gratitude for that. But being dislodged from her location in the tavern and returned to her home presented a serious problem. She couldn't do her research from here; it put her aunt at risk and it was too hard to slip away and blend in. She was far too conspicuous as a gentile lady. She would need a new plan.

The rumble in her stomach reminded her that she had slept through breakfast. Determined to continue on her quest, she rang for her maid. Food first, planning later.

When Christopher entered Lady Braxton's dining room for the second time, the scene was not unlike the first. The stately lady sat at the head of the table. Meera was nowhere to be seen. But the atmosphere was markedly different. Lady Braxton smiled readily when she saw him and the footman who poured the tea was practically bouncing.

Before he could comment, Meera entered the room like a whirlwind. "Hello Auntie!" She said cheerily as she made her way around the table. She beamed at the footman as he pulled out her chair for her. "Thank you, George. Oh, please tell me that Monsieur did not make those just for me?" She said delightedly as she helped herself to one of the sweet, freshly baked chocolate croissants laid out on a tray suspiciously close to her accustomed seat. "Not usually a luncheon food, but I will not complain. I missed the pastries most of all." She winked at George, the footman, who flushed pink before bobbing a short bow and hurrying out of the dining room.

Christopher stopped just short of rolling his eyes at Meera's antics as he took the seat directly across the table from her. But his annoyance must have been evident, for the smile faded from Meera's face and Olivia glanced questioningly between the two of them.

"You seem well recovered from your ordeal last night." Olivia said as two footmen entered the room and began serving the first course. Christopher wasn't sure who this was directed at, but he chose not to respond. Meera leapt at the opening.

"Oh yes, I am quite well. Sleeping in my own bed was a dream." Meera said, her bright smile back in place. "You never quite appreciate it until you've been away for a time."

"Indeed." Olivia nodded. "Lord Bowden, will you be staying in Paris long, or are you too missing the comforts of your home?"

Unable to dodge her now, Christopher nodded slowly. "I will stay a few days more, a week maybe. Since I am here in Paris, there are a few business connections I want to take the opportunity to explore. But then yes, I will be headed for home."

"Lovely. I will have some time to thank you properly for seeing Meera home safe." Lady Braxton smiled. Christopher groaned inwardly. The last thing he wanted to do was spend time hobnobbing with French society. Most noblewomen's idea of a *'thank you'* was some sort of ball or other social function.

"That really is not necessary, Lady Braxton." Christopher said.

"Nonsense. It is completely necessary. And I am sure I can be of some help to you. I am well connected with the noblesse and the major merchant families here in Paris. I would be happy to make introductions to anyone who would be helpful in your business endeavors." Olivia buttered a pastry for herself as she continued, "In fact, perhaps a little soiree would be just the thing…"

"No!" Meera burst in loudly. Olivia looking confusedly at her niece, her eyes narrowing. Meera usually adored parties. Christopher regarded her with curiosity; that was quite a response for a relatively ordinary suggestion. What was Meera up to?

"Pardon me," Meera said hurriedly. *Now I've put my foot in it*, she thought to herself. "Perhaps I am not as well recovered as I thought." She said with a little self-deprecating chuckle. "All I mean to say is that I do not think I am quite up for a party just yet. After the excitements of the last twenty-four hours." She added, noting her aunt's furrowed brow and Christopher's thinly veiled amusement at her discomfiture.

Olivia was sure something else was going on. But glancing between her niece and the young man across from her, she suspected it had something to do with the undercurrent that was clearly running between them. "Alright, dear, that is understandable. I will think of some other way to thank you, Christopher." Lady Braxton saw Meera cringe ever-so-slightly at her use of Lord Bowden's given name, and decided she had the measure of the situation precisely.

Christopher couldn't shake the sense that Meera was up to something, even as the main course was served and the conversation turned to other topics. He noticed that she kept her eyes mostly on her aunt. Was she avoiding making eye contact with him? Probably for the better. The spark between them last night had been lit by close quarters and adrenaline, but there was nothing more to it than that. He couldn't let there be any more to it.

Meera tried very hard to ignore Christopher for the rest of the meal. She knew he did not buy her excuses. But she did not really care; as long as he did not pry further it would be alright. She just needed her aunt to return to her normal routine, so that Meera could make plans without arousing suspicion. Well, she did love chocolate croissants. No need to fake that, she smiled and popped her third onto her plate.

Chapter 7

Madison,
I found her.

He had been sitting in Lady Braxton's library for half an hour, and that was all he had managed to get down onto paper. Christopher cleared his throat, annoyed at himself. Ignoring better judgment, he crossed to the decanter across the room and poured himself a stiff dram of brandy.

It should have been simple. He wanted to pen a letter to Madison telling her that he had found her sister, and she was healthy and whole. The letter would take a couple of weeks to reach her in London, but it seemed the least he could do. On the whole, he was not a particularly good friend to Madison and he knew it. That was probably why he felt the need to take on this mission to Paris in the first place. He owed her.

But what had started as a simple task had proven much harder. What else did he say? He could not describe the circumstances in which he had found her; that would only worry Madison more and that was the last thing she needed right now. But he was not going to lie to her either. Sitting back down, brandy beside him as an incentive, he forced himself to write more.

I found her. She has been safely returned to your aunt, Lady Braxton. I will stay a little while longer to make sure nothing is amiss.

Was that too much? God, if Madison's husband Henry thought he was upsetting her in her condition, he would be a headache when Christopher finally made it home. Unsure what else to say, he signed his name and drank the brandy.

Clunk.

He stopped just short of draining the glass. Clunk. Christopher felt the hairs at the nape of his neck rise. He had been so certain that they were not followed. Slowly he set down his glass and walked soundlessly to the door of the library. From outside, he heard a muffled sound of frustration. Could the men from last night somehow have gained access to the house, in the middle of the afternoon?

The door was heavy and he could not remember if it had creaked when he opened it earlier. Well, best to be quick and take them by surprise, he thought to himself. Without another moment's pause he swung open the door and lunged into the hall.

"Ahhhhhhh!"

"What the hell?"

"Be quiet!" Meera hissed, clutching the window ledge for support.

Damn, damn, damn. What was he doing in the library? Meera didn't think she had ever seen Christopher pick up a book.

It took Christopher but a glance to get the measure of the moment. Meera, dressed in a drab gray hood, stood at the window, which had clunked closed on the parasol that she had been using to lever it open. He stepped closer to her, looking over her shoulder and out.

"You would never have made it. The drop is too far. If you were lucky, you would have only broken an ankle." He said sardonically.

Meera gritted her teeth. "You did not seem to think anything of us climbing out of a second story window last night." She whispered.

"The second story of a tavern and the second story of a Parisian townhouse are not the same thing. Lofty titles, lofty ceilings." He motioned to the ornately adorned ceiling above them, which easily stood fifteen feet tall.

"Shhh!" The imbecile was going to alert the staff with all this jabbering, and then she would be lying to her aunt again. Meera grabbed his arm and pointed back towards the ajar library door. Rolling his eyes, Christopher leaned around her and yanked the parasol from where it was lodged in the window. He must have seen the heat rising in her eyes, because he didn't say anything else as he followed her into the library.

Checking the hall behind them to make sure that none of her aunt's overzealous staff had wandered into the hallway, Meera closed the door behind them and breathed a little sigh of relief. This was exactly why she could not continue her investigations from her aunt's home; it would be impossible to keep them out of it, especially with everyone swooning around and doting on her after her absence.

"Ahem."

Meera leaned back against the door, looking Christopher up and down. She was trying to decide what she was going to tell him. Lying was no use, he had clearly ascertained that she was trying to sneak out of the house. After last night, she thought he would be angry with her. But away from imminent danger, he seemed more amused. His dark blonde brow was arched over those piercing blue eyes, a cocky tilt that said he clearly expected her to answer for herself.

"I do not think we need to worry my aunt by telling her about this," she began.

"Don't we?" Christopher interrupted, tossing the parasol on the sofa and sitting down. He propped one foot on the opposite knee and leaned back, spreading his long arms across the back of the sofa.

"No," Meera said slowly. "She has had quite enough fright and worry over the past month, I am sure. I do not want to drag her into this."

"Fair enough." Christopher nodded. Meera began to feel uneasy.

"Well, alright then. We will speak no more of it. I will take my parasol, and..." She reached across to grab the handle and was stopped abruptly as Christopher grabbed her arm. It didn't hurt, but it was firm. He was not letting go.

"Sit down, Meera." His voice had hardened. He still raised his eyebrows as if it was an invitation but his tone was commanding.

"I will not have you order me around in my own house, Christopher." Meera bristled. She pulled her arm away, and Christopher released it instantly. She could get the parasol later, she decided, turning for the door.

"But it is not your house, is it Meera?" Christopher said. "It is your aunt's house. And if you are so insistent that she not find out you were trying to kill yourself climbing out of a window just to avoid her, then I need to know why."

"Trying to blackmail me now? You really have changed." Meera said angrily.

"Blackmail implies I have something to gain. Where you are concerned, Meera, it is sure to be nothing but trouble." Christopher motioned to the armchair opposite him. "But I have come all the way to Paris to make sure you are safe, and if you are trying to abscond the day after I find you then clearly the job is not done. So, sit down, and tell me what the hell is going on."

Unwilling to give in completely, Meera perched on the arm of the chair. "As I told you last night, I am looking into some private matters which facilitated my residence at the tavern where you found me."

"So, you went into hiding voluntarily?"

"I did not go into hiding! I was doing research! My aunt was not supposed to think that I was missing."

"Fine. Just confirming what I already suspected." Christopher said. He could tell Meera wanted to ask him exactly what he knew, but she held her tongue. "Go on."

"My investigations have not concluded. That is why I was trying to leave the house: to continue my efforts." She nodded her head sharply as if that finished things and stood up.

Christopher was unphased. If anything, he seemed to settle deeper into the sofa, making himself more comfortable. "And you needed to sneak out of the house because…?"

"Because I do not want my aunt to be involved in this matter." Meera answered tersely.

"As you have already said." Christopher was trying hard to look casual, but his insides were boiling. She looked like a goddess. Her temper was up and her dark eyes were pools he could easily remember getting lost in. Loose strands of long blonde hair were escaping her hood and framing her face. Why was she so damn enticing? How could he want to kiss her and throttle her all at the same time? He decided to focus on a spot on the wall behind her. There was a red book bound with gold striping. Maybe if he did not look at her, he would be able to hold it together until his brain caught up with his traitorous body.

"You are underestimating the danger of the situation. Those men found you last night. I do not know how, but whatever you were investigating, someone got tipped off and decided to eliminate you."

Her stubborn façade softened slightly. "I thought you said we weren't followed. How could they possibly know who I am or find me here?"

"I do not think we were. And it is entirely possible that they do not know your name or where you actually live. Probable, even. But if you keep sticking your nose where it doesn't belong, eventually someone will find out. And then you will not be the only one in danger."

"But my aunt too," Meera sank down into the armchair, realization making her face fall. Christopher chanced a glance at her. The fire was gone from her eyes, but she still looked just as beautiful. Now heartbreakingly so.

"Tell me what is going on," he said gently.

Meera took a deep breath, trying to still her swirling stomach. The last person whose help she wanted was Christopher. But anything that put her aunt at risk was not an option. Beating back her screaming insides, she began.

"A few months ago, I was at a ball with my aunt. I was returning from the ladies' retiring room and I stopped in the hallway to adjust my shoe. They were new, and weren't fitting right. As I was stopped, I overheard two voices discussing the arrival of a shipment of goods. I didn't think anything of it at first. Paris is different from London; here the merchants and the noblesse mix much more. It is not uncommon to hear people talking business."

Christopher nodded along.

"But then I heard the name Madame le Marie. I was interested; she is a friend of my aunt's. One of the men – there were two men – said that the Madame's order was sufficiently large that no one would notice the addition of a few extra items. It struck me as very odd."

"And the sensible thing at this point would have been to walk away." Christopher said drolly.

Meera pursed her lips. "I was not going to just walk away when it became clear something untoward was happening."

"You do not know that something untoward was happening. There could be a reasonable explanation."

"If you would let me continue," she glared at him. "One of the men sounded…nervous. As they talked, it was clear that he was not the one in charge. He was answering to the other man. He said the last customer had asked too many questions, and he was afraid that next time the authorities would get involved. The other man scoffed, told him it was nonsense. After that they started to move around inside the room, I could hear the chairs. I think they stood up. I knew I needed to leave. The last think I heard was the more confident man telling the nervous one to be sure to meet the delivery at the warehouse. I did not hear the exact address, but it was enough to direct me to the street in the textile district – "

"– where the tavern was located." Christopher finished.

"Yes."

"Why didn't you just report this to the authorities? Or to your aunt? Taking a room at a tavern seems like a dire step."

"The authorities can be bribed! And my aunt would have tried to put me off. She thinks I am too impetuous."

"Where would she ever get an idea like that?" Christopher scoffed.

"Stop it, Christopher." Meera's eyes narrowed. "I am perfectly capable. Just because I am a woman, does not mean I am helpless. I was not going to sit by and let people I care about get taken advantage of when there is something I can do."

Christopher felt his frustration rising again. Well, frustration was better than temptation, he told himself. "And what exactly were you able to do, Meera? Almost get yourself killed?" He said sarcastically.

"I know all of the textile merchants with warehouses on that street. I know where their offices are and the names of the men in charge of each warehouse." She rebutted.

"Something a man could have accomplished in a day or two without hiccup. But took you, a woman, weeks. And not without raising suspicions." Christopher replied.

"Well I am a woman! What do you expect?" She yelled back, livid.

Christopher sighed. Here was the old Meera: defensive, hot-headed, impulsive. "I expect you to leave a man's job to a man."

"I am just as smart and brave as any man!" She retorted.

"If only you had a little wisdom," He muttered under his breath. "Look, Meera, I am not saying that it is fair. I have no doubt that in a different world, you would have this thing figured out already. But the world does not treat men and women the same, and the fact remains that the danger to you is greater."

Meera was totally deflated. Had Christopher really just recognized her as capable? "I…thank you…" She said softly.

Christopher stood up and began to pace the length of the room. Meera observed him with interest. She could see his face working. He was muttering to himself very softly. Finally, he began talking through gritted teeth.

"Everyone outside of your aunt, Madison, and Henry think that I am here in Paris on business. Madison hasn't said anything to your parents or your sister Leonora. I already have business partnerships in Milan, Barcelona, and Marseilles. Establishing a line of business here in Paris is perfectly viable. I keep a diverse portfolio; I even own a textile manufacturer outside of Barcelona. If anyone looked closely, which I doubt they will, they would see a totally legitimate English businessman researching potential investments."

"I do not understand." Meera said.

"I will focus on investigating the textile merchants. You will keep exclusively to parties, afternoon teas, social gatherings, and French high society. Try to find out who might have made similar large textile purchases in the past few months."

"You are going to help me?" She asked in disbelief.

"I told Madison I would find you and make sure you were safe. Well, if anything has become clear to me, it is that you will not be safe until this nonsense reaches some sort of conclusion. So logically, I need to get it concluded. Then I can get out of this godforsaken city." He said brusquely, his back to her as he stopped pacing halfway down the wall of books.

Christopher nearly jumped out of his skin when he felt her hand close around his. "Thank you, Christopher." She said simply, a soft smile on her lovely face.

"I am serious, Meera. If you put yourself in danger again, I will go straight to your aunt with everything I know. This is not a game." He said firmly. Her smile faded, but she nodded.

"You have gotten much bossier in your old age." She observed, releasing his hand. Christopher felt himself let out the breath he had unconsciously been holding since the moment her skin touched his. "I accept your terms. But I want regular updates."

"Fine." He agreed. Trying to shake himself free of her intoxicating effect, he crossed over to the desk and pulled out a blank piece of paper. "Now I need you to tell me everything you know so far."

Twenty minutes later, as Meera sashayed from the room and he looked over his notes, Christopher felt confident he had gleaned as much information as possible from Meera. God-willing, whatever she had stumbled on was innocent and this whole ordeal would be over within the week. Putting the sheaf of notes aside, he picked up and reread the note he had written to Madison.

Then he drained the remaining brandy and added a post-scriptum:

She is still a pain in the arse.

Chapter 8

For the second time in his brief sojourn in Paris, Christopher was awake too early in the bloody morning, his mind clouded by the dredges of drink. Meera had insisted on daily exchanges of information. Well, he hadn't had enough time to find any new information, had he? So why was he awake?

While he was not an early riser by nature, neither was he one to lay about for half the day. His body had a natural rhythm of sleeping and waking that had always worked just fine for him. But in order to keep Aunt Olivia out of the intrigue, they had to meet early in the morning while she was out on her daily ride. So, he begrudgingly asked the valet to awaken him at first light. It was not the waking that was the problem, really. It was the wine.

Christopher could not keep her out of his head. After their encounter the afternoon before, he met with a couple of business contacts he had here in Paris. The side benefit of this otherwise arduous trip was that he could firm up lines of business that he had avoided pursuing for the last decade. He also used the opportunity to ask a few probing questions about the textile trade. While not usually a large part of his business, he was easily able to disguise the interest in casual conversation. But all the while, there she was, lingering in the back of his mind.

She was even more beautiful than he remembered. The earnest bloom of youth had settled into sophisticated beauty. The long blonde hair, which he remembered so often trailing over her shoulders and whipping in the wind, was now elegantly plaited and coiffed. As a young woman, dressing had been an afterthought, and she was radiant in anything. Now, she was intentionally dressed in bold colors and designs that not only matched her personality, but enhanced her beauty and highlighted her womanly curves. He could see the curve of her breasts and hips in his mind's eye. It was seared there. She had always been well proportioned; he remembered all too well the feeling of her beneath his hands, pressed against him in embrace. Then there was the promise of marriage; the gentle and eager exploration that he had felt sure would one day be fulfilled. And then she was gone.

As hard as Christopher tried to hold on to that anger, he could not deny the truth. He burned for her. Not the way he had, as a young, inexperienced boy. He wanted her as a man wants a woman. He wanted to feel her breasts, bare and heavy in his hands. He wanted to ravage her long, elegant throat, trace the curve of her hip with his mouth. Hence, the wine.

He gladly accepted an invitation to supper from one of his associates so as to avoid having to see Meera again, and even more gladly taken the proffered bottle of fine French wine. Alone in his room, he had drunk glass after glass, trying to drown the desire for her. Eventually he slipped into unconsciousness in the chair next to the fireplace, where he passed an uncomfortable few hours before the valet awoke him.

Running his fingers vigorously through his hair, he tried to reorient himself to the world. He looked terrible, the looking glass confirmed. Well hell, what did that matter? Maybe Meera would think twice about giving him those damn inviting smiles.

Below in the garden, Meera paced furiously up and down the hedgerow to keep herself warm. She was dressed in her heavy fur-lined pelisse, with mittens on her hands, but the chill of dawn was still thick around her. Originally, she thought this idea of meeting early in the morning quite clever; her aunt would be out riding, and the morning was the busiest time of day for the staff. No one would take any notice of her and Christopher. It hadn't even been hard to get out of riding in the morning with Aunt Olivia; she simply stated that she was not feeling up to it yet. And of course, overly concerned for her health and wellbeing, the dear older woman had just nodded with a smile of understanding.

But it was damn cold, without the heated bulk of horse beneath her and physical exertion to keep her warm. She hoped that Christopher would not dally or she might give in and wait inside instead.

Meera felt herself warm noticeably at the thought of Christopher. Oh, what a terribly frustrating, bossy, handsome, and irresistible man he had grown up to be. She had no difficulty admitting to herself that she was attracted to him. Why wouldn't she be? The part of him that had called out to her and been answered by her own body when they were young had not ebbed with time. If anything, it had gotten stronger.

She was a woman now, full grown and mature. At twenty-seven, she knew her mind and her body well. True, she was a virgin still. But she had experienced her fair share of amorous embraces and stolen kisses. She knew what attraction felt like and was not disturbed by its appearance. But what she had never felt before was the overwhelming ferocity of that attraction. Not never, she corrected herself. Not since she left England.

So, Christopher was special. She scoffed aloud at that. It should not take a genius to puzzle that one out. Of course, Christopher was special. He had been from the moment she met him. It was interesting that a decade of separation had not doused the flame she carried for him. And she carried it still, she acknowledged. For ten years, as she swam to-and-fro in the social eddies of Paris, she waited to feel that feeling again. She wondered if she ever would; perhaps it was a peculiarity of youth that was only meant to be experienced once. Then Christopher reappeared in her life, and all of those feelings came rushing back. Alright, that answered that question. The new question was… what would she do with those feelings?

Meera's musings were interrupted by the appearance of Christopher himself, clothed in a heavy wool coat against the cold morning. From several yards away, she could tell immediately that something was wrong. His shoulders were hunched forward menacingly. As he got closer, she was able to observe his disheveled dark gold hair and red-rimmed eyes. Instinctively she took a step backward as he approached.

"Good morning," she said tentatively.

"Is it?" Christopher's voice was like gravel. He shoved his hands deep into the pockets of his coat and gave her an ominous look. Meera was confused; when they left each other yesterday, things were cordial between them if not even a little bit…warm. What happened in the interval?

"I was not able to find any new information yesterday, but –" she began, but was cut off abruptly by Christopher's scoff.

"Of course not," he said acerbically.

Meera felt her dander rising. "You were the one who insisted on confining me to parties and teas. I am perfectly capable of assisting you."

"Ha, hardly. We saw where that landed you."

"Whatever is the matter with you?" She demanded in frustration.

"It is too damn early."

"Since when are you a slugabed?"

"Do not pretend like you know me." Christopher bit out.

"I do know you!"

"No, you don't." His voice was dead even, but dangerous for that.

Meera forced herself to take two deep breaths before responding. "You were out late. I assume you have some information to share."

Christopher blew his breath out of his nose forcefully, looking like a veritable dragon in the cold. But he did answer: "I met with two associates of mine who are now located in Paris. I was able to determine the names of the major players in the textile trade here. That is where I will start, under the guise of looking to expand my business investments."

Meera nodded, considering this information. As she did, the wind shifted and she got a damning whiff. She turned her narrowed eyes on Christopher. "You're soused!" She cried, voice ringing with accusation.

Christopher's own eyes narrowed. "Not anymore, sweetheart." He said sourly.

"You are not taking this seriously at all!" She cried, stamping her foot in frustration. She crossed her arms and turned away, storming down the paved walkway.

"Damnable sot," she muttered under her breath. "Self-centered, immature brute!"

It took all of Christopher's self-control not to respond. She was not as quiet as she thought she was. She stopped at the edge of a small pond, staring angrily into its dark depths. He came to stand beside her, but did not speak. He could feel the anger emanating from her like heat.

Even angry, she was like a siren pulling him in. He desperately wanted to drag her against him and show her exactly how serious the situation was for him. Damn it all, he thought; perhaps he was still a little drunk.

It was not a conscious choice, but in the next moment he had pulled her against him, hands set firmly on her round hips. He caught her lips against his, and the smoldering embers inside him lit.

Meera was so surprised, she did not react immediately. When she did start to realize what was happening, her reaction was not to pull away. It was to respond. She felt her own arms slide around his waist, comfortingly warm and solid. His kiss was intoxicating, literally and figuratively. She could taste the wine on his lips.

Christopher slid his tongue boldly into her mouth, expecting her to resist. But no tremor of surprise or distaste rippled through her. Instead, her tongue met his own eagerly and she leaned into him, her body seeking to deepen the embrace. He felt himself start to stir against her and knew that they were about to cross an invisible line. And there would be no coming back.

With an incredible force of will, Christopher pulled himself back from her. Meera looked momentarily surprised, but then started to regain herself, taking deep breaths and smoothing her skirt. She looked up at him, blowing a steadying breath out through her lips, and then smiled.

"Until tomorrow," he managed to say. Meera nodded, her eyes not leaving his. Christopher turned away, retreating towards the house. He made a concerted effort not to look back over his shoulder.

Meera watched him go, wrapping her arms around herself to hold on to the warm feeling that flooded her body, the smile fixed on her face.

Chapter 9

Christopher was frustrated with himself. He was beginning to realize that coming to Paris had been a terrible idea. He should have hired someone to come in his place. It would have been expensive, but it would have been worth any amount of money. He could feel his defenses against Meera crumbling, and they had been reacquainted for no more than a few days. She was everything he remembered and more: beautiful but not vapid, fascinating to engage with but also infuriatingly strong in her opinions. Getting himself wrapped up in her little investigation meant he had no easy way of extricating himself from her or from Paris. He would have to be around her constantly. For God's sake, he was living in the same house with her. Avoiding her was nearly impossible.

This point was borne out as he was leaving the townhouse the next afternoon. He was on his way to meet a friend of a friend at le Cercle Royale, a private gentleman's club in Paris. He was a member of his own club in London, but Paris gentleman's clubs had a particular reputation. Naturally, one had to be invited, which had not been too difficult to manage. Business was often conducted in such places. He would speak to this connection about the possibility of setting up an office for his own company here. Then he would carefully start probing to find out more information to help Meera's cause. His cause now, he supposed. And maybe then the club would provide the type of entertainment that might actually get Christopher's mind off of Meera.

He was so deep in thought, he nearly knocked Meera over on the stairs. Christopher was coming down quickly as Meera climbed them from the first floor. She was holding the handrail, but lost her balance as Christopher crashed into her and stumbled backward.

Christopher reacted without thinking. With one hand he grasped her outstretched hand, while his arm wrapped around and pulled her forward against him with force to prevent her from falling backward down the stairs. They landed with a hard thunk on the thick-carpeted stairs.

"Are you alright?" Christopher asked quickly.

"I think so," Meera said, nodding. She did a quick inventory of her body. While she was not injured, she was startlingly aware of how closely their bodies were pressed together. Their hands were clasped together tightly where Christopher had grabbed her to pull her back. She landed on top of him, so that her breasts were pressed against his abdomen and her waist was caught between his knees. Both of their breaths were coming hot and fast from the exhilaration of their near tumble. They were so close she could smell the soap of his freshly laundered clothes. It was shockingly intimate.

"You just keep on saving me," Meera said with a weak smile.

Still flush with surprise, Christopher could not help his chuckle. "I don't think this one counts. I was the one who nearly knocked you down."

Meera laughed in return, and in doing so moved her body against his. Christopher felt jolts of desire shoot through him where her soft, rounded curves were rubbing against him. Totally innocent and utterly alluring. He could feel himself starting to harden, and realized that laying as she was Meera would soon be fully aware of it as well. He released her hand and quickly lifted her off of him, setting her on the stair. As far away as he could manage.

As her breathing returned to normal, Meera studied Christopher. Was he as deeply affected as she was? This was more than attraction. This was desire. When he picked her up and set her away from him, she felt her body's instinctive cry to regain the closeness. To touch him. Christopher was doing an impressive job at keeping his face blank. Meera did notice that his clear blue eyes, which were usually bright, had taken on a darker cast. That was interesting.

"I should certainly have been paying better attention as well." Meera said, clearing her throat. "Perhaps you would allow me to repay you for saving me yet again?"

"That is not necessary, I assure you." Christopher stood up and then offered his hand to help her up as well.

She took it and pulled herself to her feet. But when Christopher tried to pull his hand away she held it tight. "I insist," she said. Their eyes met, holding them both locked in place for a moment. Then Meera had an idea. "You used to be an avid rider. My aunt has quite a well-stocked stable. Let me take you out for a ride."

"I really don't have the time, Meera. I have an appointment to keep –"

"Not now, of course. Tomorrow morning." Meera said breezily. "Not early. We can go after breakfast," she winked, knowing his disdain for early mornings.

Christopher felt a tightness in his chest. He knew he should refuse her, of course. This had trouble written all over it. But with an idiocy that he thought he'd long outgrown, he heard himself instead saying: "Alright."

"Lovely!" Meera smiled brilliantly. On a whim, she leaned up and kissed him on the cheek, like one might do to a very close friend or relative. Christopher was not maintaining such an austere look now. His expression was clearly worried. Meera decided not to press her luck any further and departed up the stairs with a farewell smile, leaving Christopher feeling completely bowled over.

Meera was not concerned when Christopher did not show up for their morning rendezvous in the garden. In fact, she did not even go out herself. She kept her maid posted at the back door to come notify her if Christopher did show up, but she thought it unlikely. He was not an early bird by nature, and they were going to be spending the entire morning in each other's company.

A little shiver of anticipation snaked down her spine. She was still wary of him; it was obvious to anyone with eyes that this man was not the same one she had known and loved all those years ago. But Meera was also fascinated by the changes in him and intrigued by her body's response to his. She was excited to see what might come of their morning alone together.

Originally, she planned on joining him for breakfast. But as it was, she spent too much time fiddling with her appearance and by the time she descended the stairs Christopher was exiting the dining room.

"You haven't eaten," Christopher observed instantly. He held open the door to the dining room for her. "Please, do go ahead. We can go for a ride another time."

Trying not to be discouraged by how badly he wanted to get out of her presence, Meera shook her head and smiled brightly. "No, no. I will be fine. I had a spot of something in my room as I was getting dressed. I am ready." She assured him.

Unable to argue, Christopher followed her down the hallway and out into the courtyard. As always, Lady Braxton's excellent staff anticipated their needs, and there were two horses saddled and waiting for them. Meera walked up to the smaller of the two, a gray-white mare, and patted her nose affectionately. Then she turned back to him.

"I hope you will not mind that I picked a horse for you. François is a sweet boy, but he does need a strong hand. Are you up for it?" She motioned to the other horse, a majestic chestnut who chose that moment to shake his mane and stomp his front hooves.

"Of course," Christopher checked the saddle, a force of habit from years of riding. He could feel Meera's gaze on him as he examined the horse. Riding had been a love they shared when they were young. Meera had always liked to ride fast. Christopher easily remembered constantly following her pell-mell on his own horse. He glanced at her, and was surprised to see a look he recognized but that was not totally familiar.

Christopher considered himself an experienced man when it came to the fairer sex. He had spent his share of time in less than reputable establishments as well as done the rounds at London's haute ton balls. The expression he caught on Meera's face was one he knew well, but that just then took him by surprise: desire.

She wanted him in the same way that he wanted her. Well, not exactly, he corrected himself. He doubted that Meera had any idea what the true implications of her feelings were, respectable society woman that she was. One thing was abundantly clear to him: he could not lose control again. It would be disastrous for both of them. He might be attracted to Meera but he certainly did not trust her. Hell, he wasn't even sure he liked her at this point.

Trying to shake off the disquiet settling into his stomach, Christopher swung himself up into the saddle. Meera took his cue and mounted her horse as well. They rode out onto the street, where the sounds of traffic made it impossible to talk. Christopher followed Meera along the wide boulevard for a block and then they crossed into the park. There were many pathways, and though Christopher had not been riding there before it was easy to recognize the small parties of French nobles promenading on foot, on horse, and in open carriages.

For a while they were able to trot and even canter, but as the park became busier they were forced to slow their mounts to a walk. Meera pulled up on her reigns so that Christopher came up alongside her.

"It's not exactly the wide-open fields of the English countryside. But the weather is fair today." She observed.

"So it is," Christopher agreed. He looked around the crowded park. "Paris is so…congested. Everywhere I go people are practically on top of each other."

Meera nodded agreement. "Realistically, one must go to Versailles or the countryside for more room to move about. That's what you get in a city that is booming since the Restoration. I haven't been to London for years, but it cannot be much better."

"No, it's not. But it's also not full of Frenchmen." Christopher said sardonically.

Meera laughed, a musical sound that made Christopher want to earn another. "What have you got against the French?" She asked.

Christopher sighed but did not respond. He cleared his throat and looked determinedly away, as if he could not stand to look at her. Then it clicked into place for Meera. It was her. She was the reason he did not like France, or Paris, or anything having to do with this place.

"I see." Meera said, almost to herself. But Christopher heard her. He glanced at her, and the pain in his eyes made Meera's heart clutch. He gave his horse a little kick and trotted ahead of her down the lane.

Meera felt disheartened, but not entirely discouraged. The past was behind them. Now that they were here, working together to unravel this mystery, they would have to build a new relationship. With a determined nod, she kicked her own horse to catch him up.

They were approaching a long, straight lane where they could see far ahead of them. And by some miracle, there were no patrons strolling or riding along. Meera urged her horse into a canter, glancing over her shoulder at Christopher as she passed him. He did not need much encouragement. He urged his mount forward and within a few moments they were both galloping full out down the lane. Neither of them could help the smiles of appreciation and enjoyment that came to their faces and were still there even as they slowed their horses down near a turn in path.

"You did quite well! I thought François might give you a hard time!" Meera panted, still reeling with exhilaration.

"Not at all – we understand each other, don't we?" He gave the brown horse a solid pat on the rump. Christopher's dark blonde hair was rumpled from the wind and framed his face, accentuating his bright blue eyes which just then were glittering with enjoyment. He sat well on the horse, his muscular things gripping the saddle and his tall body clearly in command. Meera found herself quite out of breath, but it was no longer from the exercise.

"I see you haven't lost your edge." Christopher observed. Meera blushed at the compliment.

"I love to ride. It's not the same here, but I go out every chance I get." She urged her horse forward, and Christopher followed.

"I know what you mean. Hyde Park will do when I am in London, but there's nothing to match a long, unencumbered gallop." Christopher and Meera talked amiably as they wove through the trees and made their way back to the street and into Lady Braxton's courtyard.

A groom came forward immediately, taking the reins from Christopher as he jumped down. Without thinking, he walked to Meera's horse and helped her dismount. His fingers curled around her waist as he lifted her down. Her rounded hips pushed against his hands through the layers of fabric, which might as well have not been there for all they did to quell his desire.

Their eyes met. Her feet touched the ground, but neither of them moved away. Christopher searched her dark eyes, once known so well and now a mystery. Could he trust her again? Did he dare?

Meera felt all sort of emotions and desires coursing through her as she stared into his eyes, now a clear cerulean blue. "I am supposed to meet my aunt for tea." She managed to say.

Christopher nodded and stepped back. He shook himself, almost as if trying to awaken from a dream. "Of course. I have an engagement this afternoon with a merchant who deals in textiles. I have told him I am interested in the possibility of a new investment. Hopefully I will learn something valuable." Turning the conversation to business felt much safer. Christopher gave her a small bow. "Thank you for the excursion, Meera." Then he remounted his horse and rode out of the courtyard before either of them could get into any more trouble.

Chapter 10

The next week passed uneventfully. Christopher was exhausted. He had studiously avoided Meera during the daytimes with the exception of their morning rendezvous. Which meant he had accepted a different invitation to dinner and entertainment each night, avoiding Meera and Lady Braxton but leading to late night after late night followed by early morning meetings, and days spent outside the house investigating.

For her part, Meera was equally dissatisfied. It was easy to reintegrate into the social whirl of Paris. It was quite fashionable for young women to take sojourns to the countryside to 'restore their health' and she was able to explain away her absence without much effort. But she had applied the same energy to investigating in her social sphere as she had to the Paris mercantile. Morning salons, musical luncheons, afternoon teas, evening galas and balls; each with an outfit change in between. She felt that she had not gotten a proper night of sleep since her first night home.

Of course, when she did lay down to sleep, her dreams were haunted. She had hardly seen Christopher outside of their daily check-ins. But he was always there in her periphery: buttoning his thick overcoat to go outside as she turned the corner of the stairs; dismounting his horse in the courtyard when her carriage arrived home from the evening's soiree. *Why had he kissed her? What did he want?* She asked herself again and again.

She knew she was attracted to him; and she had every reason after their multiple encounters to believe that those feelings were reciprocated. Lord, he was a confusing man. What was so difficult about acknowledging one's desires? She could certainly acknowledge hers.

After a week without progress, she decided they needed a change of tactics. And she needed a decent night's sleep. So, she invited him to have tea with her when she knew her aunt would be out playing cards with her friends, as was her routine on Thursday afternoons.

Christopher joined her promptly just as the clock chimed the half hour. He did not say anything, but nodded briefly and accepted a cup of tea.

"Well, I have talked so much about fabrics and ribbons and this satin versus that in the past week, all of my friends must think me the most boring creature in Paris. Or else about to start my own business. But I have no new information." She said without ceremony. "I am not sure this plan of yours is working."

She watched Christopher for signs of a reaction, but he simply poured a little cream into his tea and stirred it silently. Unable to bite her tongue, she continued. "We need to take more proactive action. Now, I know you are going to say that will put me in danger again, but –"

"I agree." Christopher interrupted. Meera stared at him, completely nonplussed.

"You agree?" She repeated slowly.

"Yes. Why the tone of surprise?" He said, a smirk on his face as he took a sip of tea.

"Well, I just did not expect it." She answered honestly.

"Believe it or not, I am not contrary just for the sake of it. And I do believe you capable of having good ideas…" He allowed, "Just not your ability to distinguish them from the bad ones."

"I…" Meera began, but then she bit her lip. He agreed with her. An unexpected and fortuitous surprise. Best not to take his bait.

Christopher sipped his tea again while he waited for her to continue, but when she did not he put down his cup and uncrossed his legs, a stance of business and work to be done. Meera observed him with interest; this was a different side than she had ever known: mature, careful, commanding.

"I have also made little progress. I managed to question employees at all of the warehouses, and have a general sense of how their business is run: where they import from, what kind of materials they specialize in, their typical type of clientele, and so on. So far, it all seems above board. However, there are three companies that have been more cautious: Wrighthouse-Smith, which is English-owned but does extensive business in France, as well as Expéditeurs Unis and Manufacture Royale, which are based here in Paris. They aren't evading my questions, but I am not getting straight answers either."

"Why, that's wonderful!" Meera said. "That is definite progress!"

"I would not get too excited." Christopher shook his head. "There could be any number of legitimate reasons they aren't ready to chum it up with an Englishman, from patriotism to protecting lucrative contracts. It just isn't enough to incriminate any of them." He explained. Meera nodded her understanding, setting her chin in her hand as her elbow rested on her knee. She did not realize how appealing it made her look; it was a habit. But to Christopher, it was an act of beauty: the delicately boned forearm and long graceful fingers framing clear, luminous skin and her lips, pouted out slightly in frustration. Before his thoughts could run away with him, she sat back up.

"I have been thinking about it. I believe we should give a dinner party." Meera noted his quirked brow. She smiled and continued: "Aunt Olivia and I usually entertain weekly, often more. She has not been hosting in my absence, but now that I am home people will expect us to start again or else wonder what is wrong. It is the perfect cover…"

"…for getting a specific group of people together without arousing suspicion." Christopher finished her thought.

"Exactly!" Meera smiled brilliantly, and Christopher felt something inside of him shatter. "I would invite Madame la Marie, whose name I originally overheard, and anyone else I can think of who would be likely to place a similar order. And Aunt Olivia could invite some business connections, specifically those associated with the businesses in question."

Christopher furrowed his brow. "Do you think such a specific request would make her wonder?"

Meera shook her head. "She believes that she is indebted to you, remember? If we mention that you are interested in investing in the textile trade here in Paris, she will fall over herself to make sure the right people are invited. My aunt and I have a bit of a reputation as entertainers; I think we can be sure any invitations we send will be accepted." She smiled self-indulgently.

Christopher started to imagine how appealing Meera would look, decked out from head to toe in Paris high fashion, and he considered perhaps this was not as brilliant of an idea as he originally thought.

Chapter 11

On the evening of the party, Christopher came downstairs a few minutes before the appointed time. He wanted to be ahead of Meera, for reasons he himself did not really understand. Perhaps it was because this endeavor was so firmly in her territory and sphere of influence; he wanted any advantage he could get. But he was not a stranger to high society, he reminded himself. He had almost ruined a society wedding just days before he came to Paris. Internally he cringed at the thought. He would have to do something to make it up to Madison and her friend Kelly when he returned to London.

He heard Meera before he saw her; she was giving a charming laugh in response to a compliment from the footman stationed at the top of the stairs. As soon as she rounded the curved stairway, Christopher knew he was right to be wary. She was an enchantress.

She wore a deep sapphire blue gown that was beaded with thousands of tiny iridescent black pearls.

The glowing gems were arranged in curved lines and patterns that accentuated her full breasts and generously rounded hips. She was not a debutante, confined to prim and proper pale hues and necklines. She was a cultured, sophisticated woman who knew she was alluring and was not afraid to show her self-confidence.

Meera intentionally styled her hair very simply so that the intricacy of her gown really shone. Her thick golden mane was wrapped in a tight chignon, and a single strand of dark pearls draped across her forehead before being caught in the twist of her hair in back. She watched Christopher's face and was deeply gratified to see his eyes darken with what she thought was desire.

"Good evening," she said as she descended the last few steps. Christopher reached for her hand and kissed it with a gentlemanly flourish. He seemed reluctant to let go.

"Are you ready?" He asked, his voice sounding slightly strangled.

"Yes," Meera answered, noticing that her own voice had a strange, uneven quality to it.

Christopher realized he was still holding her hand. Thankfully, the bell rang, announcing that their guests were arriving. Looking relieved, he tucked Meera's hand into his arm and said "Shall we?"

"I suppose we must," she said with a tumultuous smile, even as she felt her insides start to spin. She was a bundle of nerves and it had nothing to do with their momentous dinner party.

Lady Braxton managed to secure the attendance of high-placed gentleman from each of the three textile companies that Christopher had expressed an interest in learning more about. While she did not know any of them directly, she had a reputation as a social matchmaker of sorts. Once she put it out that Christopher was her guest of honor, and made much of his business enterprise, the invitations were quickly accepted. Monsieurs Aguillon, Daigre, and Vivier all clearly knew one another, and greeted each other coolly.

For her part, Meera invited four women and their husbands, all whom she knew socially. Alexandra of Rouen was a close friend, an Englishwoman with a French husband whom Meera had known for many years. Her husband had recently purchased a new mansion in Paris, and Alexandra was occupied in redecorating it from top to bottom. Hence, she was in the process of placing large orders for upholstery, curtains, linen, and so on. The other three women included Madame la Marie, whose name Meera had originally overheard, and two other women who were also considered *grande dames* of Parisian society: Vicomtess Marguerite and Baroness Eleonore.

"We quite missed you at our soiree, my dear," Alexandra said to Meera, who was seated across the table from her.

"I was sorry to miss it, but the country air really did do wonders for my health. I am feeling *so* much better." Meera could see that her friend was not particularly convinced by her explanation. She decided to change the subject before she questioned her any further. "Tell me, how are the renovations coming along?"

Alexandra gave her a curious look but obliged. "What a disaster! We nearly had to relocate the party because I was afraid that the ballroom would not be ready in time. We have been living in the most hideous conditions upstairs, but I wanted to put all our focus into making sure the downstairs was ready. I could not give my mother-in-law the satisfaction of seeing me fail." She laughed, and her husband rolled his eyes.

"What sort of renovations are you doing?" Monsieur Daigre asked astutely. He caught Meera's attention from the start. Of the three merchantmen, he was the only one who seemed even remotely interested in the female attendees. Monsieurs Aguillon and Vivier had been focused solely on Christopher almost to the point of rudeness. Personally, Meera thought Daigre was the most intelligent; not vying pettily with the other two men for Christopher's attention and making a favorable impression on his hosts, who were known to be Christopher's familiars.

"All of them," Alexandra's husband said sarcastically.

"It has been quite a project," Alexandra conceded with a smile. "The house is in need of complete renovation from top to bottom. I have spent a small fortune already on flooring, furnishings, drapery, you get the idea." She paused as a footman leaned over to refill her wine glass, and Meera jumped in.

"Monsieur Daigre, perhaps you could be of aid my dear friend!" Meera said. "My aunt has told me that your company works particularly in luxury textiles." Monseiur Daigre smiled at the implied compliment. Meera knew a lot more than that about his company, thanks to Christopher's investigations. But Daigre took the bait, leaning forward eagerly to talk to Alexandra and her husband.

From the other end of the table, Christopher watched the interactions between Meera, her friends, and the merchant named Daigre with guarded interest. On either side of him, Aguillon and Vivier had been talking to him rabidly all evening. So far, they had not told him anything that he had not been able to figure out on his own. He was starting to think that this whole exercise had been a waste of time. And he did not like the way Daigre was looking at Meera: like a hungry wolf. Clearly Christopher was not the only one to notice the charms wrapped in sapphire this evening.

"How long will you be staying in Paris, Lord Bowden?" Baroness Eleonore's sharp voice cut through the fog around him. Not missing a beat, Christopher turned towards the elderly woman with a charming smile.

"I have not yet decided," he said, noting that all three of the merchantmen turned their attention to him now. "It is so difficult to depart when one finds himself in such charming company." He tipped his glass casually to Lady Olivia and her niece. He met Meera's eyes, just for a moment, and felt heat rush through him. Her face flushed in answer and she immediately took a sip of wine to cover her awkwardness.

Daigre also raised his glass. He was an attractive, dark haired man approaching middle age. There was just the slightest hint of silver at his temples that had the effect of making him look more debonair. "I would like to raise a toast to our hostesses. I must say, I am surprised to find myself in such company and cannot help but wonder at my good fortune. We are such an…odd assortment this evening."

Meera blushed again, but this time not from desire. She began to speak, but Christopher interrupted her. "I confess, it is I who am responsible. I mentioned to Lady Braxton my desire to expand both my business and social contacts here in Paris, and she kindly obliged me." He raised his glass, taking clear control of the situation. "To Lady Braxton and Miss Hutton: thank you for your generosity and hospitality." There was a murmuring of agreement and then all the guests drank. The party moved on to their food and other conversations.

Meera caught Christopher's eye across the table. She mouthed a silent *thank you*, and Christopher again felt that rush of warmth that was becoming more and more familiar when he was around her.

When the women transitioned to the parlor, Meera excused herself discreetly, promising her aunt she would join them again promptly. She had not been able to calm her jittery nerves all evening. Every look from Christopher was like a draft of some heady drink – illicit, intoxicating, exciting. She walked down the hallway and let herself out onto a small balcony overlooking the gardens. She hoped a few moments of cold night air would clear her head.

Meera heard footsteps behind her and felt her heart leap in anticipation. As she turned she was startled not to see Christopher, but Monsieur Daigre.

"Pardon me," she said, quickly trying to hide her disappointment.

"No, please pardon me for intruding on your solitude, *mademoiselle*. I saw the gardens in the moonlight and could not resist admiring the scene." Daigre replied with a smile. Something about his tone made Meera wary though he said nothing inappropriate.

She forced herself to smile graciously. "Lady Braxton has curated a beautiful *verdure*, by daylight or moonlight. If you will excuse me, Monsieur, my aunt is expecting me." Meera moved towards the doorway, but Daigre stepped in front of her blocking the way.

"Please, indulge me a moment longer," he said, his gaze clearly on her bosom rather than the flowers. Meera gritted her teeth. She did not want to offend a man who might have valuable information, but she was also not going to allow him to pursue this avenue any further.

"I really must insist," Meera said firmly. She starting to step around him deliberately.

Daigre put his hand on her arm to stop her from moving past and at the same time stepped forward so that his body was a hairsbreadth from hers. He was close enough that she could smell his cologne. Meera jerked away as if she had been burned.

"Monsieur!" She exclaimed sharply. "Take your hands off of me at once!" Though by the time she said this, Daigre had already started stepping back towards the door. Rather than looking embarrassed, as she hoped he would, he looked irritated.

"Meera, is everything alright?" Christopher appeared at the open door.

Panic crossed Daigre's face and he looked quickly at Meera to see what she would do. She spoke calmly. "Yes, I just needed a bit of air. Though I do have a question for you, if you have a moment Lord Bowden."

"*Excusez moi*," Daigre said under his breath, disappearing immediately inside.

Christopher's eyes followed the other man suspiciously. Once he was gone Christopher closed the door and turned to Meera. "What's wrong?" He asked immediately.

"Nothing," Meera said, turning away. Christopher did not question her, which she appreciated. But she also knew he did not believe her answer. She sighed. "I hope you got whatever information you needed from that pig, because I do not want him back here."

Christopher cursed. "What did he do? Did he touch you?" He had his hand on the door before she could even answer, clearly intending to hunt the other man down.

"Christopher," Meera put her hand on his to stop him from opening the door. She looked up into his eyes. "I handled it. Please, let's leave it at that."

He swore again. Clearly Christopher did not want to leave it at all, but he managed to nod. "I did not like the way he was looking at you."

But Meera was not thinking about Daigre. She was caught in Christopher's bright blue eyes, now a shade of deep sapphire in the darkness. She was entranced by the warmth that spread from their clasped hands. "It's not so different from the way you look at me." She said softly.

Slowly, Christopher reached up and stroked his hand down the side of her cheek. Meera let out an involuntary purr of pleasure in response. "Tell me to stop." He whispered.

Instead she kissed him.

Chapter 12

Christopher had been walking for a long time. The park that ran adjacent to Lady Braxton's townhouse, where he had gone riding with Meera, was expansive. Over the last couple of weeks, he found himself here often. Walking by himself, he tried to make sense of things. His conversations at the dinner party the night before had been only somewhat helpful. After their guests left, he and Meera sat in the sitting room running through everything that was said over and over again. Meera confirmed that she did not think any of their voices were the same she overheard all those weeks ago. Monsieur Vivier was too much of an idiot to be running any kind of large-scale plot. That did not mean that someone in the company he worked for wasn't culpable. Daigre left before they rejoined the party – not surprising given the set-to that Meera had given him. So they really had not learned much there. Aguillon fit the bill; *slick* was the word that came to Christopher's mind. While he was clearly interested in doing business with Christopher, he was not very forthcoming when Christopher tried to probe him further. But none of it was concrete.

Still, Christopher could not shake the sense that there was something he was missing…some connection he was just not been able to make. So, he walked and walked. As he did, his thoughts inevitably turned to Meera. The attraction between them was quickly escalating. Soon Christopher feared that he would not be able to restrain himself – he would give in to his desires against the better judgment of his brain and his heart. Meera had changed in many ways; but in many others she was the same young woman he had loved before. He could feel the camaraderie, friendship, and even trust starting to grow between them again. Did he dare let it?

Meera was equally distracted. She was sitting in an upscale tearoom with Alexandra and several others from their social circle. Normally this was one of her favorite parts of the week. She enjoyed spending several long hours socializing over tea and trays of treats, admiring the elegant surroundings, being admired by other patrons. But today she could not stay engaged. She asked Alexandra to repeat herself several times. Her tea turned cold, forgotten in the gold-rimmed teacup.

Her relationship with Christopher was advancing. As they sat in the sitting room last night, talking and commiserating, things almost felt like before. They were not able to narrow down anything concrete about their investigation, but she could feel the trust growing between them. There were less barbed comments and more loaded smiles. Oh, the way he kissed her. That felt like before, but even better. She felt herself flush at the thought, and looked around quickly to see if anyone noticed. But her friends were all happily engaged in sipping and chatting. Meera decided it was time to go; she was not enjoying herself, and clearly she was not going to be missed.

She said goodbye to her friends and then waited for her carriage to be fetched. The day was cold and brisk, but the sun was shining. When Maximus pulled up with the carriage, she declined his hand up.

"I think I will walk for a while, if you don't mind." She said.

"It's all the same to me, miss," he said obligingly. Meera started down the street. She could hear Maximus and the carriage rolling along behind her. They were in a busy part of the city, and the congested streets of Paris kept the carriage more or less apace with her walking.

The cold, fresh air felt wonderful. It made Meera feel optimistic. They were getting closer to figuring this whole mess out, she could feel it. She was not sure what the next step was, but she also felt certain that together she and Christopher would be able to figure it out. What would happen then? Her optimism faltered. Then, Christopher would leave.

She was so caught up in her thoughts, she did not notice that the road was blocked by an overturned cart. All of the traffic in the street was stopped, including Maximus and the carriage. Meera kept walking, turning the corner and continuing up the next block.

Meera was jerked suddenly into an alleyway. She yelped loudly, but a grimy hand was forced over her mouth. Her nostrils were flooded with the scent of unwashed male. Terror rushed through her as she looked all around her. They were in a narrow, heavily shadowed alley. No one was visible on the street. Though she did not think about it consciously, she was instinctively aware that this was a life or death situation.

She tried to wrench herself free, but another burly arm curled around her waist. Meera felt herself being lifted off the ground. The fur trim of her pelisse caught on something, causing her attacker to falter. She jerked her mouth free and screamed as loudly as she could. Then she felt a sharp blow to her head and everything in her vision blurred.

"Miss Hutton!" Meera heard a familiar voice yelling. She was not quite sure what happened, but she felt the thick arms release her and she fell to the ground with a jarring bump. Maximus' voice came closer, and she vaguely registered the red hair of the man retreating at a run down the alleyway.

Christopher knew something was wrong the moment he entered the courtyard. The footman, Maximus, was sitting on the ground with his head in his hands. Several others were standing around him looking disturbed. The carriage was not put away, and the horses were riled. He did not stop to ask questions, but charged through the front door to find Meera and her aunt. They were in the sitting room.

He froze in the doorway. Meera was pale as a ghost. Her aunt Olivia was trying to give her a glass of water, but Meera's hands were shaking so badly that she couldn't quite grasp it. "She needs something stronger." Christopher crossed to the sideboard, poured a dram of whiskey, and handed it to Lady

Braxton. "See that she drinks that," he said before disappearing.

He reappeared several minutes later. The whiskey was gone, and while Meera was still visibly shaken the color had started to return to her face. Christopher poured himself a glass, downed it, and then repeated the story as Maximus had recounted it to him.

"Is there anything else?" He asked Meera.

"It was the same man. From the tavern." Meera said, looking directly at Christopher. Christopher swore under his breath.

"From the tavern? What in the Lord's name were you doing in a tavern?" Lady Braxton was clearly shocked.

"Aunt, please, it's very complicated –" Meera began, but her aunt interrupted her.

"I think I have been quite accommodating, my dear. But I am not stupid." She said sharply. "I know you two are keeping secrets. You are adults, it is not my job to chastise you. But this has clearly gotten out of control."

Meera stared at her hands. She did not know what to do. But Christopher saved her a response.

"We cannot tell you anything more." Christopher said calmly.

Lady Braxton's eyebrows shot up. She looked from Christopher to Meera and then back again. Christopher's expression was resolute, and Meera took strength from it. She met her aunt's eyes without hesitation.

"The situation has become more dangerous than we thought. They know who you are, Meera." Christopher said. "We need to leave Paris immediately."

Meera shot to her feet. "We cannot! If we do, all of our work will be for naught!"

"If we stay here, they will make another attempt. You might not be so lucky next time." Christopher said. He felt his temper beginning to rise.

"I will be more careful. I will not go out by myself. For God's sake, I will even let you escort me everywhere if you must." Meera insisted.

"Ahem," Lady Braxton interrupted. Meera and Christopher both looked at her in surprise. The stately older lady stood up, crossed to the sideboard and poured herself her own measure of whiskey. She downed it in one gulp, garnering a look of surprise from Meera and respect from Christopher.

"Christopher is right. I think you need to return to England." Lady Braxton said. She held up her hand to keep Meera from replying. "I thought I was being paranoid, but I have noticed the same man on the street corner the past three days. He is watching the gate, and I think he is following me. I do not know what is going on, and perhaps it is better if I do not know the details. But if someone is following me, then someone is certainly following you." She said to her niece.

Meera deflated, sinking back down onto the sofa. She put her elbows on her knees and her face in her hands.

"We can continue our investigations from England. My connections are better there, and it will be much easier to ensure your safety." Christopher said. He felt for Meera; this was not what either of them had wanted. But the situation had escalated and they were running out of options.

Several moments of silence passed. Finally, Meera's muffled response came. "Alright." She said.

Christopher did not wait for a second. "We will leave tomorrow. I will go make the arrangements now." He turned for the door.

"Maximus had best go with you as well. He knows too much." Lady Braxton said, sitting down on the sofa and putting her arm around her niece. Christopher nodded and disappeared once again.

Chapter 13

It was late by the time Christopher returned to the townhouse. He spent the afternoon and evening firming up arrangements with a few new business partners, finalizing details of their departure with Lady Braxton's staff, and posting letters to several people back in England. He let his household know they were coming. He wrote his agent in London about the new Paris deals. And against his better judgment he wrote to Madison's husband, Henry. He did not want Madison involved in this matter, but Henry was extremely resourceful and well-connected. Even if he did not like the man.

As he walked past the dining room, he felt a twinge of regret. He did not have time to return for one last supper from Lady Braxton's superb chef. Instead he had eaten a rushed meal in an alehouse. He was contemplating how much of a disruption he would cause if he went down into the kitchen in search of something to eat when he noticed the library.

The doors were closed, but there was a warm orange glow seeping underneath into the hallway. He knocked softly on the door as he pushed it open. The fire was roaring, filling the room with heat and light. Meera was sitting on the hearthrug in front of the fire. When he entered, she glanced over her shoulder but did not say anything. She reached over and tossed another log onto the fire.

Christopher did not interrupt her silence, but came and sat on the floor beside her. He leaned back against the sofa and stretched out his long legs. Meera looked different than he had seen her since coming to Paris. She was in a pale violet dressing gown that was not tied, clearly showing the frothy white nightgown beneath. Her long, thick golden hair was loose around her shoulders, completely unadorned. She looked vulnerable, young. He could almost forget that this was not the same girl he had loved in England a decade ago.

"It is a whole new world, and yet I feel much the same as I did before I left England." Meera said, almost as if she were reading Christopher's mind. He did not say anything, but his gaze shifted away from her to the fire. Meera, however, looked right at Christopher. "We are different people now."

He nodded. "That is true. We are older." They had been children, really, when they met. Meera was sixteen, not even out in society yet. Christopher was just eighteen himself. Technically of age but completely naïve about the world.

"Not just that," Meera said. Now she was studying him. There were lines and creases where once it had all been boyish smoothness. He wore his hair shorter now. But most arresting was his manner. He was not the joyous, carefree boy but a careful, serious, intense man.

"You are just as headstrong and independent as you ever were." Christopher said truthfully. Now seemed like the time for it.

"You used to love that about me."

Christopher did not respond.

"You never asked me to change or be different than I was. No expectations of a demure, retiring society debutante." Meera wished he would look at her. She wished she could read his feelings as easily as she once had. "You are different." She said again.

Christopher chuckled humorlessly. "Of course I am. At eighteen, I thought I had my life figured out. We were going to be married, make a life and a family together. But you left, and so I had to build a life for myself, by myself."

Meera bit her lip. She wanted to retort. When her Great Aunts Josephine and Olivia had visited England, she had been enraptured by their tales of traveling the continent. Until then, the extent of her travel had been between her family home and her elder sister Leonora's estate in Wales.

Her Great Aunt Josephine had been in poor health; she invited Meera to Paris as a companion to Olivia. Meera accepted the offer without hesitation. She assumed that Christopher would support her – that he would see the excitement of the opportunity and how perfect it was for her. She would spend a few years in Paris, then she would come home and they would marry. They could have everything, the best of all worlds. But Christopher had not seen it that way. All he had seen was betrayal and hurt that she could leave him and England so easily.

But there was no point in having that argument again. Meera knew that. It was a testament to how much she had grown up in the intervening years.

"Can someone that age even know what true love is?" Meera asked, frowning wistfully.

"I thought I did." Christopher said softly.

A shadow of a smile flitted across Meera's face. "So did I."

They sat in silence for a few more minutes, both staring into the fire. Then Meera reached out and took his hand.

"I hurt you when I left. I am sorry for that," she said softly, her eyes locked with his.

Christopher did not know what to say. As the silence stretched between them, he thought that perhaps at this point in their lives, ten long years later, there was nothing else to say. The past just *was*.

"Are you sad to leave Paris?" He finally asked.

Meera turned to look back at the fire. Her chest heaved in a sigh, but she shook her head. "I will miss my aunt. She has been my best friend for my entire adult life. But I suppose we both knew that it would not last forever. And to have to leave under these circumstances...it feels so unfair."

Christopher nodded, but Meera didn't notice. She was staring straight into the flames, her face full of intensity. "No chance to say goodbye to friends or to see favorite places one last time. I can't even tell the truth to the staff here, who have been like my family. I will be gone, just like that. I did that once already in my life, and I..." her voice broke, and Christopher realized there were tears streaming down her cheeks.

For the first time in his life, he believed she was truly aware of the pain she had caused when she left

England. So acutely aware that she couldn't bear the thought of causing that kind of pain to others again. And it made him ache for her. He wanted to take her in his arms and kiss away the tears.

"Perhaps…" He started to speak, but felt his own courage falter. "Perhaps we can start again, Meera. Maybe…" He struggled to find the words.

"Forget the past?" Meera said.

"No, I do not think that is realistic."

Meera nodded. "Maybe we just focus on the now?"

"We can try." Christopher agreed.

Now that it was out there, it did not sound like much. But for Christopher, just giving voice to it was hard enough. And Meera realized it. She squeezed his hand reassuringly.

"My, my, we really have grown up, haven't we?" She said, attempting a teasing tone.

"I don't know. With your hair down like this, you look just the same." Christopher flicked a lock of her hair, trying to match her playfulness. But the spot where his fingertip touched her shoulder burned and Meera swallowed hard.

"I have been wondering since you came to Paris how much you have changed." She reached out and touched his face. "Your lips, that feeling I get when we kiss…that feels the same." She ran her fingers through his hair. "Shorter, but still thick and beautiful. It looks like molten gold in the firelight." Meera knew she was crossing an invisible threshold, but she did not want to stop, "I have laid in bed, wondering what it would feel like to have your arms around me."

He did not say anything, but he did not pull away either.

"Christopher, tell me you feel the same."

Very slowly, he reached out and touched her face in the same way she had touched his. He ran his fingers through her hair, marveling at the softness. "Meera, it's all I think about."

This time when their lips met, it was slow and thorough. Every embrace so far had been fast, furious, a loss of control. This was a conscious, deliberate choice. But that did not make it any less powerful.

His fingers still threaded in her hair, he pulled her to him. She was radiating heat and it felt like fire everywhere their bodies touched. Christopher kissed her deliberately and completely, touching every corner of her mouth with his. His tongue traced the edges of her lips while his fingers massaged the base of her neck. Meera let out a little moan that reverberated between them.

She ran her fingers up his chest and over his shoulders, pushing his waistcoat down and off. Feeling his muscles under her hands separated only by the linen of his shirt sent shivers of excitement through her. The firelight made his blonde hair glow and tinted his skin golden brown. *Lord, he really is perfect,* Meera thought to herself. She started to pull at the neckline of his shirt, and Christopher caught her hand.

He wanted her so badly. But it was going too fast. He had agreed to try and separate his feelings of the past from the present, but at the moment he could not. And he worried that she would not be able to either.

"Meera…this is a hard time for you. Let's not doing anything that you will regret later." He said.

At first she felt wounded, but as she took deep breathes she realized he was right. Minutes earlier she had been crying for her loss. She nodded. But she also knew she could not stay here with him a moment longer and keep control herself. Pulling herself to her feet, she placed her hand on his shoulder. "Goodnight Christopher."

Christopher lifted her hand to his lips and kissed it softly. "Goodnight Meera."

Chapter 14

The first inn they stopped at was one where Christopher stayed on his journey into Paris. It was a long ride to get there in a single day, even more so by carriage rather than horseback. But the carriage afforded more protection, and was undoubtedly more comfortable for the four- or five-day journey from Paris to Calais.

He chose it particularly because he knew there were suites available to rent. While he had dined in the crowded common room and slept in a modest room when traveling by himself, he wanted to afford Meera a little more comfort than that. The suite would allow them a private parlor for dining, and ensure the bed Meera slept in was at least clean.

Despite the attack and their hasty departure from Paris, Meera thought she was holding up reasonably well. Christopher rode alongside the carriage rather than inside it, which meant she had plenty of time alone with her thoughts. She would miss her aunt, her constant companion and best friend. But her thoughts already turned to England and what waited there. Home, her family, and what else? She wasn't quite sure.

She waited for Christopher to arrange for the lodgings and then followed him upstairs to the rented rooms. Maximus brought up her small traveling trunk and then excused himself to find his supper and bed below. Christopher prowled through the parlor, testing the lock on the door to the hallway and pulling the window up and down before disappearing into the bedroom.

"What are you doing?" She asked, following him into the bedroom. He was dragging the dressing table closer to the window, which he threw open.

"There is a gabled roof below. It would be an easy way to climb down and out of the room if you need to make a quick escape." He nodded at the heavy dressing table, now situated below the window. "This will make it easier for you to reach the window to climb out."

"Do you really think we have been followed?" She asked uneasily.

Christopher shrugged. "We have no reason to think we will be pursued beyond Paris. But it is better to be prepared."

"I suppose," Meera nodded, taking it all in stride. Christopher was impressed by how calm she was. Most women would have been in hysterics after everything that had happened. He knew she was not immune; he had seen her fear and sorrow and loss. But clearly Meera was stronger than most women. She did not let those feelings control her. She was in a class of her own; she always had been.

He cleared his throat awkwardly. "They should be sending some food up soon. I will be back in a few minutes. Do not open the door for anyone but me."

"What if the food arrives?" Meera asked.

Christopher shook his head. "Do not open it for anyone but me." He repeated, waiting for her nod of agreement before departing.

Meera wondered what she would say if someone did knock on her door before Christopher returned. *I could just pretend I am not here*, she supposed to herself. *That would not be strange at all*, she thought, rolling her eyes. She was sure that Christopher was being overzealous; however, a small part of her was glad of it. If he was doing all the worrying, then she didn't need to.

As it happened, Christopher and the meal arrived simultaneously. A harmless looking kitchen maid appeared and set the table before laying out an offering of stew, bread, cheese, and sliced sausage. There was also a pitcher of ale and bottle of wine.

Christopher had changed his clothes; he was dressed more casually than she had seen him, in breeches and a cream-colored linen shirt that was open at the top. A tantalizing triangle of chest was visible where he hadn't fastened the top two buttons. Meera chastised herself for salivating, and it was not because of the aroma of the food.

"Are you hungry?" Christopher asked, pulling out her chair politely.

"Starved, actually." Meera took the seat and started to tuck into the food immediately. She saw Christopher look at her curiously. "Well, it's not as if the maid is going to come back and serve us," she said with a smile, heaping food onto her own plate and then his. It was by far the most intimate meal they had shared, seated only a couple of feet away from each other rather than far across her aunt's formal dining table.

"At least the food is decent, though nothing to compare to the fare served at your aunt's table," Christopher commented, taking an exploratory bite. "Not quite as fine as you're used to."

Meera laughed. "Fancy French food is nice, but I am still an English girl deep down. Meat and potatoes will do for me just fine." She took a hearty bite in demonstration.

Christopher chuckled, pouring them each a glass of wine. Meera took a deep drink. "I will miss French wine, though."

"I think we can find a way to keep you supplied. England is not exactly the wilderness, sweetheart." He used the endearment casually, but it was like a tripwire. It set something off between them, and all of the sudden the tone shifted from light-hearted and casual to something much headier.

They ate in silence for a while, before Meera asked quietly: "Where will we go, once we land in England?"

"I have been thinking about it," Christopher said, thoughtfully fingering the wine glass he held. "I thought London at first; I certainly have the most resources there, and Madison is there. But it also isn't as secure. It is easy for something to happen and have it look like an accident. Or for someone to follow us unnoticed. We will be safer in the country, with less people and less variables."

"Home, then?" Meera looked both wistfully excited and also apprehensive. She had not seen her parents in a few years, when they visited in Paris. She looked forward to seeing them. But she had not seen the home where she had grown up since she left England all those years ago.

"No, not yet. I think it would be better if no one knows we have returned, at least for now. It will make it harder to find us, if someone is looking or following."

"Fair enough, but then where do we go?"

"Shipford Hall." In answer to her questioning look, he continued: "*My* home."

"I didn't know you had a home." She said stupidly. Realizing how strange that sounded, she added: "I meant a home of your own. I assumed you were with your brother, or your parents…" she trailed off, not knowing what to say.

"I bought Shipford Hall a few years ago. I may be the younger son, but I did not plan on living off of my brother forever." His tone was a little defensive.

"Christopher, I didn't mean it like that," she reached across the table and caught his hand. He did not stop her, but he also was not sure how to respond. Meera apparently wasn't either, for she sighed and stayed silent.

"I always knew you were meant to do something, to be someone." She finally said.

Christopher could not help smiling a little. "You were sure about yourself, that's for certain. Your opinion of me varied." He said teasingly.

"Depending on how ornery you were being at the time," Meera smiled back, not letting go of his hand. She squeezed it lightly, and then turned it over, studying the palm. She slowly traced each finger from base to tip. Every place she touched burned like a brand. It was as if she was drawing her mark, claiming him as her own.

"Shipford Hall," she repeated the name. "Tell me about it." She did not release his hand.

Christopher cleared his throat and began to talk. He described the long drive that ran along a small lake, draperies of willow trees hanging overhead. He told about how it cleared suddenly and the road dipped down into a small valley, where the house was nestled invitingly. He explained how the first time he rode out and looked down on the house in the valley, he was stunned; how he decided right then to purchase the property, no matter what state the house was in.

Meera started at his hand, but slowly trailed her fingertips upward. She traced the edge of his sleeve where it circled around his wrist. She slipped her finger underneath the linen cuff and lightly touched the tender inside of his arm. Then she pulled her hand up and ran her fingertips up his arm outside of his shirt, letting her fingernails drag slightly so they left a tingling trail in their wake. When she reached his shoulder, she left her hand there and reached up with her other hand to cradle his face. Christopher stopped talking.

Meera made a decision while she was riding alone in that carriage all day. She was a grown woman, she knew her mind and her body. She might have no idea what the next weeks held, but she knew what she wanted right here, right now.

"I cannot wait to see your home," she said honestly.

Christopher stared into her dark eyes, torn with indecision. Who was he? Who was she? Certainly not the people they had been. Were they compatible now? Maybe, maybe not. They were just starting to get to know each other, or rather, to get to know the person the other had become.

Slowly, Christopher reached up and cupped his hand around hers. He drew her fingertips to his lips and kissed them very softly.

"Did you cry when you left England?" Christopher was afraid to hear the answer. He wasn't sure which response would hurt more.

"No." She answered. Christopher felt his heart clench like a vice had been placed around it. Meera sighed softly. "I cried when I left you." And then her lips were on his: hungry, searching.

The intensity between them was unrestrained. Meera moved so she was sitting in his lap, her round bottom nestled on his thighs. Christopher felt himself begin to harden as she shifted so she could slide her arms around his shoulders and kiss him more deeply. He accepted her unspoken invitation, running his hands along her ribcage and cupping her breasts. She tensed momentarily, and then sighed as he began to massage and stroke her. Her nipples hardened against his palms, a tantalizing tease through the fabric of her dress.

Meera did not hesitate. She reached around and pulled loose the ties of her dress. Her lips never left his as she shrugged the garment down around her hips and began unlacing her corset. She wanted his hands on her skin, without the layers of muslin between them. Christopher moved her hands away and finished unlacing the corset himself. He tossed it away and took her heavy breasts in his hands, thinking he might lose himself on the spot when she let out a moan of pleasure. He wanted to push her further, he needed to know what she sounded like when he touched her. When he lowered his lips to her nipple, she cried out and plunged her fingers through his thick hair, holding on for her life.

As he trailed kisses between her breasts and along her neck, Meera started moving her hips against him. She was not sure what drove the desire, but she wanted friction, contact, closeness. The action nearly undid him. Christopher slid his hands underneath her soft bottom and hoisted her against him, carrying them both to the bed. They met the mattress in a tangle of clothing and limbs. Meera needed to feel him against her. She pulled off her stockings and petticoat and then started fighting with his shirt. Chuckling, Christopher kissed her deeply. When he pulled away a minute later, he had managed to remove the last of his own clothing. She stared up at him, panting, her body arrayed before him like a piece of art. His stomach and his heart clenched with longing and desire.

"Are you sure about this, Meera?" Christopher forced himself to pull away from her. It took every ounce of his self-control, but he intentionally moved away from her on the mattress so that a few inches of empty air separated them. He knew he had no chance of thinking clearly while pressed against her from lips to toes.

"Yes," she murmured, reaching for him, trying to close the space between them.

Christopher caught her hand, kissed the knuckles, but held her away so she could not touch him. "Meera, I do not know if you have been with other men, but –"

"I haven't," she interrupted. She could tell that he was a little surprised by that declaration. Well, she certainly wasn't behaving like a virgin. "I have been courted, of course. Perhaps I have not been the picture of virtue, but…" She was struggling to get coherent words out. Little surprise, given that her entire body felt like it was on fire. A most delicious, engulfing, fire.

She took a deep breath before continuing. "Christopher…I am not naïve. I know what attraction and desire are. I want this. I want this now, with you." Meera could see the tremor that went through him.

Unable to speak, Christopher did the only thing that seemed possible. He kissed her. Gently, searchingly, with all the emotion and anticipation and hope and fear of a decade between them.

They felt every place where their skin touched, from the tips of her breasts against his chest, to the hairs on his long, sculpted legs. Christopher did not think he could wait much longer. He slid his hand downward, and was relieved and aroused to find her entrance wet and waiting. She was serious when she said she was ready. He gave her one last, long look, giving her the chance to change her mind. But she pulled him down to her and kissed him hard. Then she raised her hips to meet his, and there was nothing between them but their own desires.

Chapter 15

Christopher was only vaguely aware of what was happening. He was still asleep. Or at least, he had been asleep. Slowly, he became aware of a rhythmic thrust of hip, soft and warm but eager; of lips leaving a damp trail behind his ear and along his collarbone; of silky locks tickling his face, chest, and then thighs. By the time he was fully awake, they were both spent, their legs intertwined and Meera letting out a deep sigh of contentment.

"If you insist on waking up early, that is the most pleasant way to do it." He observed, his fingers tangled in her long blonde hair.

She stretched against him, arching her back and limbs. Then she rolled onto her stomach, setting her chin on his chest and looking up into his eyes. "We should have been doing that from the moment you came to Paris." She said frankly.

He did not even try to suppress his chuckle. "Really?" He slid a hand down her back and squeezed her round bottom. "If I did not know for a fact that you were a maid until last night, I would accuse you of being unchaste."

Meera rolled her eyes. "Any woman who denies enjoying making love either has a bad lover or is lying." She declared.

"Touché," Christopher acceded. "Since you did not deny it, then I must be an excellent partner." He grinned.

Rolling her eyes again, Meera shifted off of him and sat up. Christopher followed suit, standing up and walking to the window, where he peered out to get a sense of the time of day. "It is still early. If we leave soon, we will be able to make it more than halfway to Calais by the end of the day." He did not pause to wait for a response, but started pulling on his breeches and searching around the room for his shirt.

Meera nodded her agreement to his plan, and started dressing herself. She pulled open the trunk that Maximus brought up the night before, smiling to herself as she noted the unused nightgown that lay on top of the other garments.

As she dressed, Christopher disappeared into the parlor and then out the door. She heard him descending the stairs, she assumed in search of something for breakfast. She had purposefully packed simple gowns that she could manage without a lady's maid, and so by the time he returned she was fully clothed and sitting at the dressing table brushing out her lengths of shimmering hair.

Christopher was temporarily stunned. Watching her bring the brush methodically through her hair again and again entranced him. For ten years, he had tried to push away the thought of her, to fill the void she had left. Last night, he made love to her. It was all he dreamed about, more even. But where did that leave them now, in the dewy light of the morning?

Catching sight of him over her shoulder in the mirror, Meera looked over at him questioningly. Christopher cleared his throat before responding:

"The maid will bring up tea and some food shortly, and then we will be on our way. Are you done with your trunk? I can take it down to Maximus to load onto the carriage."

"Yes, just one moment," she quickly plaited her hair into a simple braid, tied it with a bit of ribbon, and tossed the brush into the trunk. Christopher nodded, latched it closed, and picked it up handily. He headed out the door without further comment.

"Christopher?" She called, following him from the bedroom to the parlor. Frozen in the doorway with her trunk balanced on his shoulder, he turned around slowly, eyebrows raised.

"Perhaps you would join me in the carriage, today?" She asked.

Christopher stared at her for a moment, his face blank. Then the corner of his lips twitched, ever so slightly. "Of course," he answered.

Meera thought that Christopher would return and join her for breakfast, but after several minutes of sitting awkwardly by herself she concluded she was on her own. She picked at some sausage and sipped her tea, but she was too impatient to eat much else. She took a few scones off the tea tray, wrapped them in a cloth napkin, and stowed them in her reticule. With a quick glance around the room to make sure she'd collected everything, Meera fastened her traveling cloak and headed down into the tavern. Most of the patrons in the main room were still asleep, clearly having imbibed heavily the night before. Meera was glad when she emerged into the fresh air outside.

Maximus was hitching up the horses, but Meera did not see Christopher.

"My lady," Maximus stopped what he was doing and bowed. "Are you ready?" He offered his hand to help her into the carriage. Looking around one last time for Christopher, but not finding him, Meera accepted Maximus' hand and climbed aboard.

The carriage belonged to her aunt, but at Christopher's request it was the least extravagant of the three she kept in Paris. He insisted it would make them less recognizable. It was a chilly morning, and even wrapped in her heavy cloak Meera was soon digging out the blankets that were stored beneath the forward seat. She wrapped one around her legs and tucked her hands neatly underneath. She could have asked Maximus to pull down her trunk so she could fetch her gloves, but she did not want to inconvenience him.

The coach gave the telltale forward lurch as the horses started to walk, and then they were off. Meera did not have time to frown; there was a loud thump outside the carriage door, it swung open, and Christopher climbed in. He landed quite hard on the seat opposite her.

"Sorry about that," Christopher smiled sheepishly at her astonished look. "I told Maximus to get a move on, but he thought I would be riding again today and assumed I would just catch him up."

Meera bit her lip to keep herself from laughing, her nervous energy almost getting the better of her. "I am sure you've given Maximus quite a fright." She managed to say.

Christopher did not restrain his laugh. "I'm sure I have," he agreed.

Neither of them was sure what to say or do next. Meera fiddled with the blanket on her lap, and Christopher looked first at her and then out the window at the nondescript countryside. The ease of the morning, when they awoke entwined in each other's arms, seemed to have evaporated. Meera felt awkward and a bit worried; did he regret their night together, now that he'd had a few minutes to himself to clear his head?

There was a jolt in the road that knocked them both off balance and their knees bumped onto each other. Meera leaned forward automatically to brace herself against the carriage seat, and as she did her hands brushed Christopher.

"Lord, Meera, your hands are freezing!" Christopher exclaimed, catching her hand in his immediately. He pulled his gloves off and grasped both of her hands in between his, sandwiching them with warmth. Meera cleared her throat, and Christopher suddenly became aware of how much closer they were than just a few moments ago. He felt his chest tighten.

"You are always so warm," Meera commented. She swallowed thickly, feeling her heart starting to beat faster. "I am a trifle cold this morning. Would you come warm me up?" She glanced towards the open seat beside her.

Christopher felt himself immediately start to respond to her invitation. She had not meant it as a double entendre, but of course that was where his mind and body went straightaway. She's new to all of this, he reminded himself as he took the seat beside her. Meera scooted closer to him and spread the blanket so that it was draped over both of their legs.

Meera felt the heat begin to spread through her body, though she knew enough at this point to realize that it wasn't just the heat of Christopher's body, but her own amorous desires that were warming her now. Their hands were no longer clasped, but their sides and legs were pressed together beneath the blanket. Christopher moved his hand so that it rested on top of her leg and then slid it slowly up and down along her thigh. A delightful shiver of anticipation ran down Meera's back.

She moved her own hand slowly over his leg, enjoying the way his muscles tensed at her touch. Emboldened by her desire and memories of the evening and morning past, Meera slid her hand across his lap to where he was hardening. She cupped the growing bulge and Christopher gasped involuntarily. She may not know exactly what she was doing, but she understood his reaction just fine. Slowly she began to explore, stroking the hard length of him through his breeches, which were stretching tighter by the second.

Christopher was quickly losing his capacity for coherent thought, but before he completely lost his sanity he knew he wanted to make Meera squirm just as she was doing to him. In a bold motion, he tossed the blanket aside, rucked up her skirt, and pulled her atop of him so she was straddling his waist. Meera was surprised but did not protest, instead taking advantage of their closeness to finally kiss him.

Only temporarily distracted by her assault on his lips, Christopher pushed her heavy cloak back around her shoulders and loosened the back of her gown just enough to pull down the front and expose her breasts. He tore his lips away from hers and lowered them to one rosy nipple, puckered and hard in the cold air. His tongue drew circles around the little bud while his hands cupped and then stroked. He made love to her beautiful round breasts with his mouth until she was moaning and rubbing her hips urgently against him.

"Please, Christopher," she moaned. He needed no further encouragement. He unfastened his breeches, pulled down her hips, and entered her. She cried out so loudly Christopher was afraid Maximus might stop the carriage. He covered her mouth with his own in a passionate kiss. They moved together along with the rocking of the carriage. The sensation was so strong, Meera almost couldn't stand it. As they crashed to their climax, their lips broke apart and they both cried out so loud Maximus must surely have heard them. But neither of them cared.

Meera collapsed forward into Christopher's arms, resting her chin atop his head as both of them caught their breaths. Christopher said something, but it was muffled against her chest. Running her hands through his shining gold hair affectionately, she leaned back so she could see his face. "What was that?" She asked.

"I said," he grinned, "Neither one of us has to worry about being cold now." Laughing, he pulled her down and kissed her again.

From there, the days melted together. En route as they were from France to England, there was nothing they could do to advance their cause or further investigate. So instead they occupied the silence with stories. Over the course of days in the carriage, meals in taverns, and eventually aboard ship, they talked. Slowly they filled in the blanks of the last decade. And at night, they made love. Passionately, unreservedly, without guile or pretense.

As their carriage wove its way across the English countryside, Meera felt her worries slowly begin to creep back into focus. A visceral part of her responded with glee to the muddy roads, rolling green hills, and misty rain that made the British Isles so distinct. Nothing about England had changed, and yet she felt she was a different person, a stranger. She was still impulsive and stubborn, as Christopher was so quick to point out. But she knew herself better; could recognize those characteristics as both strengths and weaknesses. She had seen more of the world, something she always yearned for as a girl. And she also knew that in all the parts of the world she had seen, she had never felt what she did sitting right here, in a carriage in the English countryside, next to Christopher.

Chapter 16

Christopher was a bundle of nervous energy all morning. It had been almost two weeks since their departure from Paris. And now they were within a stone's throw of Shipford Hall, his home. Meera could feel him almost vibrating with anticipation. As the road curved, a small, glistening lake appeared. It was lovely, exactly as he had described it.

Christopher nervously watched Meera as they rounded the bend and the main house came into view. *Why was he nervous?* He thought. What did he possibly have to prove to Meera? *Nothing*, he reminded himself. And if she did not like his home…that did not matter either, though the thought made his stomach clench uncomfortably. They had spent the weeks between Paris and England in a daze, a fantasy world. And he had carefully avoided thinking about what might or might not happen beyond that. It was simply too painful of a road for him to go down.

Nonetheless, he could not help the surge of warmth he felt in his chest when he saw her lips curve into a small, unprompted smile.

As the carriage approached the main house, they could see staff filing out and lining up neatly. Even at a distance, Christopher was able to recognize the butler and housekeeper. *Good*, he thought to himself, *the house would be in good order for their arrival*.

The carriage bumped to a stop, and Christopher handed Meera down. She seemed completely calm, a brave smile fixed on her face. He introduced her to his butler first, an older man named Rhodes whose bearing suggested a military background. Meera greeted him politely and then followed Christopher down the line.

"This is Mrs. Adams, my housekeeper." Christopher motioned to the person directly beside Rhodes. The curly-haired, middle-aged woman bobbed a slight curtsey to Meera, but her eyes were clearly skeptical of this new arrival.

"How do you do?" Meera said politely to mask her unease.

"I am well, my lady," the woman said, still watching Meera closely. Mrs. Adams reached up to tuck a stray curl of hair behind her ear and something clicked in Meera's mind.

She was struck with an odd sense of familiarity. "Have we met before, Mrs. Adams?" She asked.

"Indeed, my lady. I was a lady's maid to Countess Bayfield when his lordship was young." Mrs. Adams seemed impressed that Meera had remembered, and her cool skepticism warmed a bit. "You may have known me as Dorothy then, my lady."

"Yes, I remember! I believe you helped my mother and I dress for the winter pageant one year. I remember you were most creative with the costumes." Meera beamed at the memory. Mrs. Adams flushed slightly at the compliment and even offered Meera a tentative smile. When Meera turned to continue, Christopher was giving her a strange look, but then his face cleared and he offered her his arm.

He led her through the main hall and into a sitting room, where a maid was hastily laying out the afternoon tea service. The young woman dipped a quick curtsy and then disappeared without a word. Meera looked around with interest at everything she saw. This was Christopher's home; the one he had built from scratch to please no one but himself. What clues would it give her to fill in the picture of the man he now was? The décor was understated; there were no loud colors or ostentatious furniture. But her Paris-educated eye told her everything was of the highest quality. She was beginning to think she had underestimated his success as a businessman. To afford a home such as this, the large staff who all lined up to greet them, and maintain what appeared a massive property…Christopher was not just doing well; he had amassed a personal fortune.

Christopher handed her a cup of tea and then sat down. "What do you think?" He asked quietly.

"It is beautiful, Christopher." She said simply. Christopher blushed, an impulse which horrified him. Sputtering into his tea, he tried to cover his embarrassment, but Meera's perfect lips just curved into a knowing smile. "Now that we are here, what are our next steps?"

Thankful to be talking about something else, Christopher cleared his throat. "I have been thinking about that for a few days. I have a friend who works with the constable at Southampton. It is less than a day's ride from here. Now that we are back in England, I think it is time to take what we know to the authorities."

She nodded. "Do you think they are more trustworthy here, than in Paris?" She wondered aloud.

"Not always," he conceded. "But I trust John unequivocally, and he will be able to advise us on what our best course of action is now."

"Alright," Meera agreed. "In the meantime, I will write to my sisters and my parents, and let them know we have returned."

"No, I don't think you should."

"Why not?"

"I told you when we were still in France, it is better if no one knows yet that we have returned. It will give us more space to investigate."

"But certainly 'no one' does not mean my own family?" Meera protested. "How can I help you if my being here is a secret?"

"You won't be investigating, that is part of the point." He saw Meera's eyebrows shoot up. He tried to keep his own temper on hold. "Paris was your arena, I admit that. But this is mine; this is my home and these are my people. No one here will betray us, and you will be safest if as few people as possible know you are here. It is only temporary, until we have more information." Meera pursed her lips, but did not immediately argue. Christopher took it as a good sign.

She was fighting with herself; she did not appreciate being dictated to, but she could also see the logic in what Christopher was saying. Finally, she nodded her head once, sharply. "Alright. I will not write to Madison, Leonora, or my parents. I will keep a low profile. For now," she said firmly. "But you must keep me apprised of what you find out. Just like in Paris. We are still partners."

Christopher nodded, "Agreed." He said, and Meera felt herself relax a little.

"Good, now that we have that settled, how about you show me around the rest of this beautiful prison of mine?" She said sarcastically, but as she took his arm she leaned up and pressed an intimate kiss to his neck that sent shivers all the way down his spine.

Several hours later, Meera sat alone in front of a mirror. She was in a beautifully appointed room, decorated in pale blues and grays. She and Christopher passed a lovely afternoon strolling the grounds and touring the large manor house. They enjoyed an informal supper, not even bothering to change into evening attire. Then Christopher excused himself to his office, saying he needed to check on a few urgent business matters. Of course, Meera let him go without protest. She was left standing at the bottom of the stairs in the entry hall. Not knowing what else to do with herself, she came upstairs to the room that Christopher had shown her earlier and said would be hers while they were here.

And now she was sitting here alone. She changed out of her dress into a nightgown. She unplaited and brushed her hair. She looked around the room and felt so…lonely. For a moment she was surprised at herself. She was fiercely independent, singularly autonomous, that was how she defined herself. And yet…in just a few short weeks, she had become very used to having Christopher at her side. Not just for meals or teatime, but for the small moments. Pulling back the bedsheets, making love, falling asleep in each other's arms.

Meera looked around the room, surveying its emptiness, and decided to take matters into her own hands. She pulled on her robe and headed barefoot out the door. It was late; they had lingered over dinner. She did not think she would meet any of the household staff in the hallways. And if she did? Well, Christopher said his staff could be trusted to be discrete.

Silently she padded down the stairs, through the main hall and past the dining room towards the back of the house. She recalled exactly where Christopher's office was from the tour he gave her of the house earlier. As she approached, she was pleased to see light shining from underneath the closed door. Good, he had not gone to bed yet. She was not entirely sure she could find his bedroom in the labyrinth of hallways on the second floor. Gaining confidence, she pulled open the door.

Christopher looked up in surprise from where he was seated behind an ornately carved cherry-wood desk. But his were not the only eyes on her. Seated across from him was a thin, dark haired man about Christopher's age, neatly attired and wearing spectacles. Meera's eyes went as round as saucers.

"Miss Hutton," Christopher cleared his throat awkwardly. "May I present my associate, John Purdue. He is the friend I spoke about earlier."

Meera knew she was blushing from her hairline all the way down the long-V of skin exposed by her nightgown and robe, right down to her bare toes. With as much dignity as she could manage, she nodded politely and crossed her arms firmly across the front of her body. "It is a pleasure to meet you, Mr. Purdue."

"You as well, ma'am," the poor man croaked. He was also embarrassed, his eyes flying between Christopher and Meera.

Christopher was trying very hard not to laugh. Meera's intent could not have been clearer as she stood in his doorway, hair loose and the rounded curves of her body barely covered by her nightclothes. But he was not ready to let her off the hook yet. "Please join us, Meera. I just finished relaying to John everything that we found out during our time in Paris."

"That isn't necessary," Meera said quickly. "I am sure you can tell me about it yourself later on." She started to back towards the door.

"Nonsense. As you have said, you are involved. Now that you are here, you should hear what John has to share firsthand." The dare in Christopher's eyes was obvious. Well, Meera could not be called a coward. Eyes narrowed, she closed the door and walked to the seat next to Mr. Perdue, adjacent from Christopher, without another word. She made a show of arranging herself in the chair and then turned her intoxicating dark eyes to the other man.

"Do go ahead, Mr. Purdue."

John Perdue looked as if he wanted to run from the room. He wanted nothing to do with whatever drama was playing out between the two of them. But his loyalty to Christopher won out. "I was about to tell Christopher that I am actually relieved to hear his news. We have received some strange reports that seem to fit the criteria you have described, centered out of Southampton."

"Really?" Meera leaned forward in excitement, uncrossing her arms and making her voluptuous chest more visible than ever. John swallowed audibly. Christopher tried not to roll his eyes.

"Y...yes." John continued. "We have several suspects who we are interested in investigating more, but lacked sufficient evidence to give us grounds to do so. I would like to take the information you have given me back to my superiors. I think we will be able to narrow down our list of suspects, and possibly even bring some in for questioning."

"That is wonderful!" Meera exclaimed.

Christopher was not as excited. "John, if you take this information to the constable, you will have to reveal where you go it from, correct?"

"Yes. Otherwise it would not be credible."

"I would rather Miss Hutton not be mentioned."

John looked at his friend with confusion. "It will be difficult, given the nature of the information you have given me, to exclude her – "

"John," Christopher said very seriously. "Her name cannot be associated with any of this; neither publicly nor privately." Meera looked on with furrowed brow; she did not understand Christopher's insistence, but his voice was deadly firm and she did not want to question him in front of his friend.

"Alright. It can be managed." John agreed, looking at Meera with renewed interest that had nothing to do with her attire. "My only condition is that you do not undertake any more investigation until you hear back from me. I do not want to risk alerting the suspects we already have."

Christopher nodded and then looked at Meera, who quickly nodded her agreement as well.

"Very well, then." John stood up, reaching across the large desk to shake Christopher's hand. "It is late, but I think the constable will want to hear this information before the morning. Goodnight, Christopher," he turned to Meera and bowed, "Good evening, Miss Hutton."

Meera smiled and murmured a farewell as Christopher stood and escorted his guest from the room and to the front door, leaving her alone in the office. She was perched on the edge of his desk when he reentered the room a few minutes later. She did not look up, but stared at her hands as she fiddled with a letter opener she had picked up off the desk.

"Ahem," Christopher cleared his throat. "Well, now you know everything that I know."

"You did promise to keep me updated." She said, still not looking at him.

"I only received word that he was available this evening just before we sat down to supper."

"Why didn't you tell me?"

"I was going to tell you."

"When?"

"When I came upstairs to your room."

Meera's head snapped up. Christopher's eyes locked onto hers. Their usually piercing blue was dark and cloudy, a look she had begun to recognize in the past few weeks. He took a step closer. Meera set down the letter opener, placing her hands on either side of her on the desk. "Why did you ask Mr. Purdue to keep my name out of his report?"

Christopher casually shrugged off his jacket and tossed it over the back of the armchair. Then he started to slowly unbutton his own shirt. "I do not want any of this getting traced back to you now that we are in England. It is safer. And, I would not want rumors about us to start getting out. What would London society think?"

Meera laughed out loud. "You know I do not care one iota what Paris or London society thinks of me."

"That must be true. Because why else would you be down here, dressed in your nightgown?" Christopher asked, slowly moving towards her. His eyes slid down her body, taking in every seductive detail.

"I was looking for a book to read." She claimed innocently, but the corners of her lips turned up in the slightest smile.

"Really?" Christopher was close enough to touch her. For a moment she was afraid he wouldn't. But then he reached out and put his hands on her shoulders. Slowly, he ran them down the length of her arms, covering her hands where they were planted with his own much larger ones.

"Yes, I couldn't go to sleep. I was…distracted." She said, feeling her heartbeat start to race and her breath coming fast.

"Distracted?" Christopher moved his hands to her thighs, pushing her legs apart so that he could come to stand between them. Sliding his thumbs back and forth along the inside of her thighs, he kissed the skin just below her ear. "It sounds like you were looking for me," he whispered.

Meera could feel her desire building. Lord, she was going to let him take her right here on his desk. "And what if I was?" She managed to whisper back.

Christopher laughed huskily. Then he slid his hands under her bottom and hoisted her up so her legs were wrapped around his hips. She put her arms around his neck instinctively as he kissed her thoroughly. "Well, Miss Hutton, you found me. Now I think it is time to remind you of where my bedroom is," he whispered into her ear as he carried her out of the room.

Chapter 17

"Where are you going?"

Meera froze bent over at the edge of the bed. She had been rummaging around in the tangle of discarded sheets and clothes, trying to locate her nightgown and robe from the night before. Finally spying them, she reached down and snatched them up. "I am going back to my room."

"Have I done something to offend you?" Christopher said lazily, not moving an inch from where he lay in the bed.

"Maybe," she said coyly as she attempted to find her way back into her nightclothes. "You do not seem overly worried." She observed to his prostrate form.

"After last night, I am feeling pretty confident." He said with a grin. Meera couldn't help blushing as she tied her robe securely around her waist. She sat down on the edge of the bed, leaned across and kissed him. She loved waking up in his arms. She loved how natural it felt between them: a caress here, a teasing word there. In fact, she loved kissing him so much she was tempted to crawl back into bed right now.

She moaned regretfully but pulled away.

"Where are you going?" He asked again, this time the frustrated desire evident in his voice.

"I haven't had a decent ride since we left Paris," she said, holding up her finger to stop him from speaking. "No crude jokes, sir." Meera admonished.

Christopher bit his tongue just in time. *Lord*, his handsome face with that half smile was her undoing. Somehow, she managed to pull herself away from the bed and took two steps back to avoid getting pulled back in. "Now, if your stable is as well appointed as the rest of the house, I am sure I will find a suitable mount?" She asked, graceful eyebrows arched.

"Several," Christopher said.

"Good. Who should I ask for?" She started towards the door.

"Never mind," he said, dragging himself up. "I will come with you."

"I –" Meera started to put him off, but stopped. "That would be lovely." She said with a smile. She did not need to be independent all the time, she reminded herself.

Twenty minutes later, Christopher strode out of the house towards the stable expecting to locate his head groom and request his horse and the one he had in mind for Meera saddled. As he rounded the corner, he was surprised to see Meera already standing there. She was attired in a very stylish emerald green riding habit, artfully trimmed with black velvet piping that accentuated her waist and the curve of her hips. It was a stark change from the simple gowns she had worn while they traveled. Her blonde hair was coiled at the nape of her neck and caught up in a woven black net that he was already envisioning removing so that he could wind his fingers through her hair. She stood next to a tall, dark bay mare, petting its nose and making friends.

"I see you have met Olympias." He observed, coming to stand beside her.

"Yes, indeed." Meera smiled as the horse nudged her arm for more attention. "I described my needs to your stableman, Mr. Arnold, and he seemed to think she would do nicely."

"She's a sassy lady," Christopher observed, noting that his head groom, Mr. Arnold, had chosen exactly the horse for Meera that he had been thinking of himself. "You two should get along." He added.

Meera rolled her eyes and laid her head against Olympias' strong neck. "Forgive him, he is still learning how to deal with strong women." She said to the horse.

Christopher ignored her comment as his own horse was brought up. He gave Meera a leg up into Olympias' saddle, said a few words to the groom, and then mounted himself. "I am surprised to find you already down here. I thought I hurried." He said.

"I was rather excited at the prospect of riding. The maid was quite put out that I wouldn't let her fuss over me more." Meera said as she walked her mount alongside Christopher's. Slowly they made their way out of the stable yard and towards the open grounds that surrounded Shipford Hall.

"This is you not being fussed over?" He made a point of looking her over from head to toe and letting his appreciation show. Meera felt her stomach do a little flip.

"One of my larger trunks arrived from Paris. Aunt Olivia must have seen it on its way the same day we left. I admit, I was very pleased to see it." At the time, Meera had been annoyed at the maid for insisting on styling her hair and fetching the coat that matched her dress from where she had been pressing it. But as she basked in Christopher's admiration, she decided it was worth the time. Feeling truly relaxed, she surveyed the rolling hills and forested nooks of the estate before her. "Where shall we go?" She asked with delighted anticipation.

"Try to keep up," Christopher said with a ready smile, urging his mount to a gallop.

She followed him eagerly as he reined his horse off of the path and into the thick green field. Meera could feel Olympias' hooves digging into the soft turf as she lengthened her stride. She leaned over her withers, assuming a practiced posture. Though the scenery around her was beautiful, Meera's eyes were focused solely on the man riding gracefully in front of her.

They rode for about a quarter of an hour before they slowed their horses amid a copse of trees. Christopher led the way, winding through the thicket of branches until they opened to a secluded clearing. He brought his horse along to one side of the clearing and then dismounted. Meera did the same.

"When I first bought the estate, I would spend hours just riding around aimlessly, trying to get to know the land." Christopher said as he tied their horses reins to a sturdy looking tree.

"That is very romantic." Meera observed, her tone teasing.

"I was trying to figure out if I had made a good investment." Christopher replied, but he quirked an eyebrow in acknowledgment. "It was the first time that I ever had something that was truly my own." He turned and walked along the edge of the clearing, and Meera watched him with fascination. Christopher always seemed so sure. Years ago, it had been the naïve confidence of youth; he had blind faith in himself, in her, and in the young love they shared. His belief in love and relationships had clearly not recovered. But throughout their trials in and flight from Paris, and as he spoke of all his business dealings, he was very confident and self-assured. Not naivete now, but knowledge and self-reliance. Interestingly, they were the same traits she was most proud of in herself.

Meera followed him, slipping her hand into his as they walked. "I never realized you felt that way." She said honestly.

"For a long time, I did not realize how I felt. You were all that mattered; I didn't really think much about what my future would be beyond us. But then you left." He shrugged, his face clouding. Meera felt a jab in her stomach but didn't say anything. "With you gone, I had to focus on other things. I figured out what was missing from my life, and I made deliberate moves to fill those holes."

Meera nodded. She could sense that things were not as easy between them as they had been when they first woke, or even when they started on their ride. Whenever he talked about their past, Christopher seemed to erect a protective wall around himself. Sometimes that manifested as sarcasm or stoicism, and sometimes as anger.

They stopped to watch a couple of birds flitting around through the weeds. She laid her head on his shoulder and spoke softly. "Half of my heart was so full, so complete, because I had you. But the other half…it just pulled me away. I wanted to see what else there was in the world. And when the opportunity came, I didn't pass it up." Meera sighed. She knew it was useless to try and explain away the past, but she could not help trying. "We were so young." She added, her voice almost a whisper.

The birds flew away, and Meera turned to Christopher. She raised her hand and traced the edge of his face. She studied his perfect, bow-shaped lips, his straight nose, and finally his striking blue eyes. "I cannot take back the past. And I am not sure that I would. The years have made us different people…better people. All I know is that today, you are exactly what I want."

She kissed him. Put her arms around his neck and pulled him to her forcefully, pushed her tongue into his mouth and thrust her hips forward in an unspoken demand. She tried to dismantle the wall between them the only way she knew how. She tugged him down to the ground, guiding his hands to her breasts. Taking the hint, he pulled at the buttons of her jacket and slid his hands inside to caress her soft skin. He tried to leverage himself onto an elbow above her, but she pushed him down onto his back. With singular intention, she unfastened his breeches and straddled him. He was ready for her. Their bodies joined in a burst of intensity and after only a few passionate thrusts they both lay spent on the ground.

Meera laid with her head on Christopher's chest, enthralled by the sound of his heartbeat and the rise and fall of his body beneath hers. She did not hear the sound of hoofbeats approaching until Christopher sat up suddenly. Following his gaze, she saw the horse and rider appear at the far edge of the clearing.

"It is Mr. Arnold." Christopher said, brow furrowed. He had told the stable boy where they were headed. The lad would have told Mr. Arnold where to find them. Christopher straightened his clothes and then stepped in front of Meera to shield her from their visitor so she could do the same.

"Sir, Miss," Mr. Arnold bowed quickly. "I am sorry to disturb you, Lord Bowden. A message came from London, and the house staff said you left word that if any notice came you wanted to know immediately…"

Christopher nodded. "Yes, I did. I did not expect to hear anything so soon," he turned to Meera. "I doubt it is anything serious, but I should go back to be sure. If the information is important, I may need to pass it along to John immediately."

"Of course," Meera agreed. She had sufficiently straightened her clothes, though she was terrified of what her hair might look like.

"I hate to cut your ride short so soon. I know how much you were looking forward to it." Even as he said it, Christopher was already striding back towards where their horses were tethered. Meera followed him without hesitation.

"I am fine," she said honestly, already relishing the idea of giving Olympias free rein. "You go back to the house. I will stay out for a while longer and then find my way back."

Christopher stopped just short of mounting his horse. He turned back to Meera. "I expected you to be running back to hear whatever news it is," he said in a slightly skeptical voice.

"And pass up the opportunity to finally be on my own, free and in the open air for the first time in months? Not likely," she reached up and kissed him quickly on the lips. "But I expect a full report when I return."

"Fair enough." He helped her into the saddle. "You're sure you do not want Mr. Arnold to stay with you?"

"I am sure Mr. Arnold has much better things to do than follow me around. Off you go," Meera said, waving them away. Reluctantly, Christopher waved and urged his horse into a trot. *What trouble could she possibly get into here on the estate?* He told himself as they rode away.

Meera had no sense of how long she was out riding, but she was sure it must have been at least an hour since Christopher and Mr. Arnold left her. The estate lands surrounding Shipford Hall were quintessential English countryside. As she rode through the familiar landscape, recognizing flowers and trees not by name but by look and feel, she felt as if she really was home.

It was so restorative to be on her own, outside and not worried about who was watching. She rode pell-mell down long straight lanes, feeling the wind rushing through her hair. Then she trotted leisurely through stands of trees. She could have stayed out forever, if not for the fact that her stomach was starting to rumble for luncheon. With a sigh and an internal promise that she would take up her early morning riding habit again, she turned back for the house.

She heard a loud blast, and then suddenly she was on the ground. The force of the impact knocked all the wind out of her and for a few moments she could not move or breathe. She had been thrown from a horse before, though it had been years. She forced herself to take a few deep breaths. As she did she became aware of the sharp pain radiating from her knee. *Damn.* She laid on the ground for several more minutes, assessing the damage to her body in general. Adrenaline would dull all pain for a few minutes; it was best to lay still until it drained off and she could be sure she was alright. After a while, she sat up slowly. She was relatively sure it was just her knee. Definitely a bruise on her hip where she had landed. But other than those injuries she was relatively unharmed.

As Meera looked around, she saw that Olympias had fled a few hundred yards away. What could have startled her? Meera surveyed the surrounding area but saw nothing obvious. She was on a well-worn path that led back to the main house. The area around her was wide-open other than a small stand of trees in the opposite direction of where Olympias now stood. One thought immediately came to Meera's mind – the loud blast had almost sounded like a gunshot.

It has been years since she heard a single gunshot – in Paris she mostly heard celebratory volleys at court. She had not heard the sound of a lone rifle since hunting with her father before she left England. But why would someone be hunting out here? Christopher told her the grounds were not open to the public. A poacher was possible, but seemed unlikely. She did not think any local game was in season. That left more insidious possibilities.

No, she told herself firmly. She was overreacting. Anything could spook a horse. She knew that as well as anyone. The whole reason Christopher brought her here was because it was the safest place for them. It just was not possible that someone could have followed or found them here. She could already imagine Christopher's face when she told him what happened and the thought made her cringe. If he suspected for a second that someone had taken a shot at her she would never be allowed outside of the house again.

Well, maybe by the time she got back he would have an update that would make the whole thing moot. That's what she would do, she decided. She would wait to hear his update, and then decide what to tell him. There was no need to worry him until she had more information.

She managed to get to her feet and then whistled hopefully. Olympias looked up. Meera whistled again, and the horse thankfully decided to come to her. By grasping the saddle and gritting her teeth, Meera managed to get herself back aboard. Her knee ached with every step Olympias took. Sighing deeply, she urged the horse slowly back towards the house.

Chapter 18

As it turned out, when Meera returned to the house Christopher was not there. Mr. Arnold informed her that when they returned, Christopher went inside for a few minutes, then came back out, remounted his horse, and said he was going into town. Well enough, Meera thought. She did not have to make any excuses.

Mr. Arnold look concerned when she told him she had been thrown from Olympias. He remarked that it was quite unusual; while she was known to be spirited, the horse had never thrown anyone before. But he seemed to accept Meera's explanation of a sudden, unexplained noise. More importantly, he acquiesced to her request not to say anything to Christopher about it.

A footman helped her hobble up the stairs to her bedroom, and a maid helped her change out of her riding habit and bathe. Thankfully they brought luncheon up to her room. By the time supper rolled around, she still had not seen or heard from

Christopher. Meera found herself getting annoyed. He could have at least left word for her about what he was up to. She should have just come right back with him that morning, she chastised herself. Then she would know exactly what was going on, and her knee wouldn't be sprained.

Meera thought they were making real growth in their relationship; they were both being more vulnerable with one another. Lord knew their physical relationship was blooming. But they were also supposed to be partners in this investigation. And being left alone without a clue did not make Meera feel like a valued confidant.

With more help from Christopher's gracious staff, she eventually made it into the dining room. She knew she would not be able to hide what had happened from Christopher. She could hardly walk. Despite her frustration with him, Meera knew she had to tell him about her fall and her suspicions behind it. By the time he walked through the dining room door to join her, she was sore and irritated.

"I was beginning to think I would be eating by myself." She said frostily, eyebrows raised.

Christopher sighed. He did not seem to notice her tone of voice. "I did not know if I would make it back in time myself." He said as he sat down at the head of the table.

"Where were you?" Meera asked directly. Hungry, sore, and impatient, she was past the point of mincing words.

Christopher opened his mouth to respond, but was interrupted when the door to the dining room opened. A footman entered the room with the first course. They sat in awkward silence as the young man served them. Then the butler, Rhodes, stepped forward to pour the wine.

"Thank you," Meera said graciously.

The stately middle-aged man nodded. "Please let us know if we can fetch anything for your knee, my lady, or to make you more comfortable."

"What's wrong with your knee?" Christopher said instantly.

"Nothing," Meera gritted her teeth.

"Then what was Rhodes talking about?" The butler looked back and forth between them, aghast.

"It is nothing." Meera insisted. The tension between them was rising. Christopher had ridden hard to get back to the manor in time to dine with Meera. To and from London in a day was not an easy prospect. He had to switch horses midway, had barely eaten, and for all his trouble had not really gotten any information of value. His temper was short.

The butler poured Christopher's wine and backed out of the room quickly.

"What is going on, Meera?"

She ignored him. He had been gone all day, without word or update, and he was angry with her? "What message did you get? It must have been important."

"Not as important as telling me what the hell is going on in my own house."

"You told me you would keep me apprised of anything you found out. I promised to lay low, to not talk to my sisters or my family, but you are supposed to tell me what is going on!" She threw down her napkin in frustration. "You could have left a note telling me where you were going. You could have sent word that you did not know when you would be back. Anything!"

Christopher's eyes darkened dangerously, and though Meera knew him well enough by now to recognize the warning she did not heed it. "It was a message from my business manager in London. I rode hell for leather between here and London so I could meet with him today. And when I get back, you are hiding things from me. Again." His voice was dangerously low.

"Hiding things from you?" Meera echoed. She shook her head in disbelief. "You still don't trust me."

"Well, it seems like I am right." He said coldly. "What aren't you telling me?"

"If I could storm out of this room right now, I would." As it was, she had to settle for glaring at him across the table. "I was thrown from my horse. I sprained my knee. I am *fine*."

Christopher was sharp enough to read between the lines. There was no reason for her to keep her injury from him unless there was more to the story. "What aren't you telling me, Meera?"

Meera almost told him everything. The sharp sound that in her paranoia she thought was a gunshot, the painful limp back to the house, how hurt she was that he did not think to let her know where he had gone or why. But her anger won out. "Tell me what you found out, or I am going to bed." She said stubbornly.

He stared at her for a minute, then leaned back in his chair with his arms crossed. "Goodnight." He said. Christopher watched silently as a footman appeared, helping Meera to her feet. He felt a twinge of regret and sympathy as a grimace of pain crossed her beautiful face. But he determinedly kept his mouth shut.

Chapter 19

Meera took every meal in her room for the next three days. If she was to be characterized as stubborn and headstrong, she might as well live up to the reputation. She wasn't really able to walk anywhere unassisted, and she was not going to run into Christopher in the hallway and be unable to walk away from him. However, by day four she was extremely bored. Her maid graciously brought her up books and writing paper from the library. She flipped through the books, reading a few pages here and there. She wrote several letters to her sisters and parents, but they all ended up crumbled in the waste bin. When her maid came to help her bathe and dress, Meera tried to engage her in conversation. But she got the sense the young woman was a bit in awe of her; in any case, her responses were mostly confined to "Yes, my lady" and "I am not sure, my lady."

She had eaten breakfast and was sitting alone by the window. In the last several days Meera had memorized this view. She watched for a glimpse of Christopher, but her room overlooked the western gardens and apparently, he did not spend any time there. She knew it was time to venture out again; it was a nice room, but not nice enough to spend the rest of her life in. And Christopher *must* have an update by now, which he was obviously withholding.

Very carefully, Meera used the windowsill to pull herself to her feet. She tested her weight, and though her knee still hurt it did not buckle under her. She took a few slow steps leaning along the windowsill for support and then a few more across to the edge of the bed unsupported. Good enough, she decided, fixing her eyes on the door.

The door opened and Christopher heard Rhodes enter. "I will take tea in the sitting room." He said without looking up from the ledger in front of him. The butler muttered something acceptable and left. Christopher sighed deeply, wrote a note at the bottom of the page, and then pushed it aside. He had spent the last few days closeted in his office. He'd been away for so long there was plenty of work to attend to and fill the time. It was also a convenient excuse to avoid running into Meera, though he was relatively sure she had not left her room in days. His butler uncomfortably informed him at meal after meal that Miss Hutton asked to have a tray brought up to her room.

Christopher was baffled at himself. In the past decade, his work had been his only real passion. He relished the hours of solitude with proposals, reports, and ledgers. He enjoyed spinning it all into a successful enterprise. But right now, the silence felt suffocating.

Well, then he would go somewhere that was not so silent, he told himself. He would go to the sitting room, throw open the windows, and listen to the sounds of birds and horses and whatever else while he drank his tea.

He opened the door of his office and walked down the hallway. As he approached the front of the house, he saw the sitting room doors were open. *Good, tea was already laid*, he thought to himself. But as he walked into the room, he realized that was the least of it.

Meera was standing with the footman, looking exceedingly awkward. Clearly, she had realized that the presence of the tea service indicated Christopher's imminent arrival. They stopped talking the instant he came in. The poor young man looked between the two of them, clearly not sure what to do. Christopher gritted his teeth. So much for a loyal staff. A week in his house and the ever-charming Meera had managed to divide their loyalties.

"You may go." Christopher said directly. The footman glanced at Meera, who nodded and gave an encouraging smile. He bowed to his employer and left quickly.

Meera's smile faded the instant the young man left the room. She sat down on the settee, carefully controlling her face to mask the jab of pain in her knee. She reached for the teapot. She poured two cups of tea, added the precise amount of cream that she knew Christopher liked, and then offered one to him wordlessly.

He took it and sat down opposite her, steeling himself for battle.

"I demand an update." She said, her calm and even voice belying her words.

Christopher reached up behind them and opened the window. There was a rush of cool breeze, and the distant sound of hooves and voices from the stable.

"I do not have any update." He said, his tone matching hers.

Meera's façade faltered. She let out a frustrated sigh and bit her lip. Christopher immediately imagined that it was his teeth that caught her full bottom lip, nipping them softly. Over the past days, as he slept alone for the first time in weeks, he debated with himself whether taking Meera into his arms and his bed had been a mistake. Now as they stood toe to toe, he knew that it made staying mad at her that much harder.

Clearly trying not to lose her temper, Meera spoke again: "Christopher, I am sorry that we quarreled, I truly am. But to purposefully keep information from me is not right. This has been my affair from the beginning." She hated that it sounded like she was pleading.

"I am telling you the truth." He saw her eyes get glassy, filling with emotion and maybe tears, and he felt like he was being stabbed in the stomach.

"We have been here a week! You expect me to believe that in all that time, Mr. Purdue has not contacted you? That your jaunt to London had nothing to do with our investigation?" She was losing her cool. Angry at herself, she turned away. She hated that he could still get this reaction out of her. Perhaps she let herself get too close to him too fast.

Christopher grabbed her upper arms and spun her around. "Why won't you just believe me? Why do you have to make everything more difficult?" He said in exasperation.

"Why can't you just trust me?" Meera retorted. She saw the pain in his face, and she knew the answer. Because after all these years, after the weeks they'd spent getting to know one another again, he was still hurt.

Neither of them was certain who initiated it, but Christopher's hands loosened and suddenly they were embracing. Their kiss was desperate and needy. They were both searching for what they missed over the past few days – the connection, the closeness, the escape from more serious considerations of their feelings.

He lowered himself onto the settee next to her. He stroked the small of her back as he trailed kisses along her jawline and at the base of her ear. Meera moaned. She slid her hand beneath his jacket, drawn like a magnet to the heat of his chest. She felt him begin to peel away the neckline of her gown and for once Meera was the one who pulled away.

Christopher did not protest. He pulled his hands back into his own lap. They were at a stalemate. Neither one of them was sure of the way forward. They sat like that, unable to look at each other, until they heard a commotion in the hall.

"Maddie!" Meera tried to leap to her feet when she saw her sister, who did not even pause in the foyer long enough to remove her traveling cloak. But her knee really only allowed her a slow hobble. Madison didn't seem to notice as she crossed the room and embraced her sister.

Astonished, Meera drew back in surprise. "Darling, are you...?" She pushed back the cloak and felt a smile start to spread across her face.

"What?" Madison looked confused, unfastening the heavy garment and handing it to the waiting footman.

"You're with child!" Meera exclaimed in delight.

"Well of course I am!" Madison looked from Meera over to Christopher, who rose from where he had been seated with Meera.

"Why, you must be six or seven months gone!" Meera exclaimed, clasping her sister's hand tightly.

"Eight." Henry said as he appeared in the doorway behind Madison. "And running mad across the countryside without a second thought." He added with clear exasperation.

"Do try to be a better loser, my dear." Madison said over her shoulder as she sank into a comfortable brocade chair. "But surely you knew. Didn't Christopher tell you?" She looked past her sister to where he stood.

Christopher shrugged nonchalantly. "It didn't come up."

"It didn't come up?" Meera said incredulously. "We've spent the last two months together, endless hours talking and...." her voice faltered for a moment as she just stopped herself from finishing her sentence. "It didn't come up?" She repeated.

"Ahem," Madison cleared her throat. "Talking *and?*"

Meera had the good grace to blush. Madison looked hard at her sister and then at Christopher, but seemed to think better of saying more on that topic.

Instead she laid back in her chair and folded her hands neatly on her rounded belly. "Well, that's a man for you." She said sarcastically.

"But what are you doing here? How did you even know that I was here?" Meera looked back at Christopher in confusion.

Henry was the one who answered. "Well, Christopher's letter was cryptic, but I did as he asked and looked into a few of my family's business connections. Given the tone of your letter, I thought it was better to bring you the information in person. But of course, Madison insisted that she come along." Henry frowned at Meera. "Didn't Christopher tell you?"

Madison snorted in a most un-ladylike way. "Apparently you could fill books with things Christopher chooses not to tell me." There was an awkward silence at that. Meera sighed and decided to ignore Christopher altogether.

"Oh Madison, you do look well!" Meera clasped her hand in excitement. "How do you feel?"

"Like a whale."

Christopher snorted quite ungentlemanly into his teacup. Meera rolled her eyes. "Well, you are a beautiful whale." She told her sister.

"It is nice to hear it." Madison said.

"I tell you how beautiful you are every single day!" Henry exclaimed, nearly spilling the tea he was pouring.

"You have to tell me I am beautiful." Madison quipped.

"I don't remember that in the vows." Henry returned.

Now Madison rolled her eyes, almost a perfect mirror of her sister a few moments earlier. "Speaking of vows, I believe I promised you I would have a lie down as soon as we made it here. I have seen my sister, so I suppose I will allow you to browbeat me into having a nap." She beckoned her husband forward, who looked a little relieved as he helped her to her feet. "We will catch up later this evening." Madison promised her sister, giving her hand a farewell squeeze. "Christopher?"

"Yes?"

"I expect we have a lot to talk about as well." She said.

"If you say so," Christopher raised his cup in salute as Madison was escorted from the room by her husband.

The evening meal was an awkward affair. As was his habit when trying to control a difficult situation, Christopher arrived in the drawing room well ahead of everyone else. Madison arrived on her husband's arm at the appropriate time, looking well rested and refreshed. She had Meera's same long, luxurious blonde hair, though she styled it more simply. She was usually a slimmer version of Meera, but her pregnancy had filled out her curves. Christopher had never really been attracted to Madison, but he could certainly understand the adoring look in Henry's eyes.

Meera waited until the very last moment to make an appearance. In fact, her maid was standing watch in the kitchen so she could summon her only when the beginning of the meal was imminent. She entered the drawing room at the exact same moment that Rhodes came through to announce it was time to be seated.

Meera dressed herself purposefully, and when Christopher's eyes lit on her she knew she had done well. She chose a gown of deep plum, with a low neckline and cinched waist. It was not really a style that was in fashion and she would not have worn it out in Paris. But she knew that Christopher adored her figure; he commented on it many times during their lovemaking. And she wanted to knock him off balance, distract him, as much as possible. She felt it was her only chance of getting him to share whatever information he had gleaned, from Henry or elsewhere.

Of course, Christopher knew what she was up to. She looked damn delectable and she knew it. Worse, her strategy was working. He wanted to pull her into his lap and whisper whatever would make her happy while kissing that soft spot behind her ear.

Instead, Christopher determined to ignore her entirely. He and Henry barely managed to be cordial to one another; so that really only left Madison. Meera made idle talk with Henry, but she kept one ear open to the conversation between Christopher and her sister. Several times, Madison turned to Meera and tried to draw her into the conversation, but Meera stubbornly resisted by giving a clipped answer and then turning back to Henry.

By the time the last course had been cleared away, all four of them were feeling the strain.

Madison wasted no time cutting through the awkwardness. "All right, Henry, I think it's time for you to share whatever information is so secret it has to be discussed in person."

Henry looked dubious. Christopher cut in: "Madison, I really do not think you should be involved in this."

Madison's eyebrows shot up. "You know he is going to tell me everything as soon as we get to our bedchamber," she said pointedly.

Christopher frowned, but Henry put his hands up in surrender.

"I do not really know what is going on myself." Henry said. He turned to Christopher. "I asked my business manager to look into the three companies whose names you sent me. It was difficult to be discreet; our family really doesn't have any textile holdings. But of the three you sent, only Wrighthouse-Smith does dealings in London, Paris, and Southampton."

"Wrighthouse-Smith," Meera repeated, frowning. She looked to Christopher. "You promised Mr. Purdue you wouldn't do any more investigating. Have you learned something new?"

"You have all the same information I have," Christopher said with annoyance. He had told her that this very afternoon. "I do not intend to renege on my promise to Mr. Purdue, I will not give us away. I wrote to Henry before we left Paris."

"What is all of this about? Textiles? This is why you left Paris?" Madison interrupted, looking confused and worried.

"Madison…" Henry began in a warning tone, but Christopher cut him off.

"Neither you nor Henry needs to know any more, Madison. Trust me on that." His tone was dead serious. Henry nodded solemnly. He did not want his wife involved in whatever nefarious business this was.

And since she would expect him to tell her everything he knew, he did not want to be involved either.

Madison looked in frustration between her husband and Christopher. She looked to Meera for help, but for once Meera agreed with Christopher. She absolutely did not want her sister to have anything to do with this business.

"Fine." Madison stood up, tossing her napkin on the table. "Meera, let's leave them to their brandy and *men-talk*." She exited the room without acknowledging either Christopher or Henry. Meera stood up more slowly, but she followed her sister.

She paused at the door. "I expect you will keep me apprised." She said coolly, leaving before Christopher could respond.

"I really cannot tell you what is going on." Meera said as they entered the sitting room.

"I don't really care about that." Madison said dismissively. She sat down and beckoned for Meera to join her. "I want to know what is going on between you and Christopher."

Meera was startled by her directness. She also had no idea how to answer her sister's question. What *was* going on between her and Christopher? When they left Paris, she might have said they were friends. Certainly they were lovers. But now? She was not sure that either was really an apt description for the state of things between them.

"It's complicated." Meera said truthfully.

"Of course it is," Madison could not help laughing. But she kept her eyes expectantly on Meera.

Meera sighed as she sat down beside her. "I was startled at first, to find him so changed from the young man I knew. But as time has gone on, I'm coming to think perhaps he has not changed as much as I thought."

"What do you mean?"

"He doesn't trust me."

"Well, can you really fault him for that?"

Meera felt as if she had been slapped. "That is not fair."

Madison was undaunted. "Fair or not, Meera, it's the truth. Christopher is a different man now. When you left, he took all that pain and anger and channeled it into building a life for himself. And he has not given his heart or his trust to any woman since."

"You sure seem to know him well." Meera said, feeling a twinge of resentment.

"I do. I stayed." Madison said simply. Meera did not reply, but got up and walked to the window. She stared out into the dark, with her back to her sister. After a few minutes Madison spoke again. "Have you shared his bed?"

"How could you possibly know that?" Meera asked incredulously.

Madison cocked an eyebrow. "Call it a married woman's intuition," she answered with a wry smile. "I do not know what is wrong between you now, but you should mend it or you should move on."

"You make it sound like this is all my fault."

"It's both of your faults!" Madison said, clearly getting annoyed. "Christopher has not been a perfectly behaved gentleman, I will give you that. But he is a good man and I trust him with my life and yours, which is why I sent him to Paris in the first place." She took her younger sister's hand tightly in her own. "Meera, I love you with my whole heart. You are brave and adventurous and stubborn to a fault. But I do not want to see you both get hurt again if this isn't going to work out."

More confused than ever, Meera pulled her hand away. "I think I need some sleep. I will see you in the morning." She gave her sister a very quick hug and then made a hasty exit from the room. As she climbed the stairs, her eyes filled with tears, but not from the throbbing ache in her knee. What should she do now?

Chapter 20

The next morning, Christopher once again sat alone in his office. He asked for breakfast to be sent in, but he didn't touch it. He could not bring himself to sit down at the desk and start working either. It was early; the morning was still dewy and wet as he peered out the narrow paned windows. He heard the door open and his heart leapt as he saw the flash of blonde hair. But as she stepped into the room he realized it was Madison, not Meera. *Damn*, he thought to himself. He was so hungry for her he literally could not see straight.

"Good morning," Madison said with a small smile. She glanced around the room. "I hope I am not interrupting your breakfast, or work, or...?"

Christopher scoffed. "Or nothing," he said. "I am surprised you are awake this early."

Madison shrugged. "Pregnancy does strange things to one's body and mind." Without asking, she picked up a piece of his toast and nibbled at the corner.

Deciding it was to her liking, she took a bite and settled into one of the chairs across from his desk.

They sat in companionable silence for a few minutes before she spoke again. "What are your intentions with Meera?" Madison asked.

Christopher gave an exasperated laugh. "If only I knew."

"Do you intend to court her? Marry her?" Madison continued when she saw the surprise on Christopher's face. "You've already bedded her, so this must have crossed your mind."

"Madison!" He exclaimed, shocked at her candor.

"Oh Christopher, do not look scandalized on my behalf." She said dismissively. "You do not need to explain yourself to me. But good Lord, Christopher, please be careful with her."

Christopher frowned as he pondered Madison's warning. "You're saying I'm not good enough for her." He finally said, his voice flat.

Madison sighed deeply. "No, Christopher. I am saying I do not know if she's good for you."

Christopher looked up in surprise. Madison cocked an eyebrow. "I love my sister dearly. But I know what happened all those years ago, and I know how badly you were hurt. Both of you."

"I am not the same person now."

"That is true. Nor is Meera." Madison conceded. "But are you both different enough to not repeat your mistakes?"

Christopher felt his chest tighten. It was the question he had been asking himself over and over again since they left Paris. He was beginning to think maybe they were ready to make a go of it, but then they argued so stupidly and it seemed like they hadn't actually made any progress at all.

Suddenly he couldn't sit anymore. He strode over to the window, opening out onto the vast fields of Shipford Hall. For so long, he thought the only real joy he would find would be here, as master of his own life. But then Meera slipped right in, charming his staff, understanding his goals and passions, as if she belonged here all along.

"I love her." He said quietly. "I don't think I ever stopped."

Madison didn't reply, but came to stand beside him and take his hand. They stood like that for several long silent minutes, staring out, until footfalls outside the door announced their reverie was about to be broken.

She gave his hand a squeeze. "Then I guess there is nothing to do but make it work."

Meanwhile, Meera had been awake for hours. She woke before dawn. Unable to fall back asleep, she dressed herself in a riding habit and then sat watching the sunrise and waiting for the hour when the grooms in the stables would wake. Her knee was still sore, but she did not care. She needed to get out of the house. When she finally judged that the hour was late enough, she silently made her way downstairs. She was surprised to find Henry in the foyer, adjusting his boot.

"Good morning. I did not expect to see anyone else up and about this early." She said as she joined him. "You are dressed for riding."

"As are you," Henry observed. He opened the front door and held it for her, motioning her through.

The morning was bitterly cold, but Meera did not feel it at all. "Perhaps we can ride together; now that you are back in England we will have to get to know each other better." Henry said with a good-natured wink as they walked towards the stables. Meera could not help smiling; her sister's husband was a charmer, that was sure. She'd been looking forward to being on her own, but she also couldn't think of a polite way to turn Henry down.

Ten minutes into their ride, Meera was ready to admit she was enjoying herself. Henry was clearly an accomplished horseman and thankfully he seemed more intent on riding than on talking. For a long time, they did not speak at all other than quick exchanges about where to go. The sun was starting to burn off the morning mists when they slowed their horses to a walk along the same road where Meera had hobbled home earlier in the week.

"Madison mentioned that you liked to ride, but she did not tell me you were such an equestrian." Henry complimented her.

Meera laughed. "She does not know the meaning of the word. As much as I love to ride, my sister hates it."

Henry laughed as well. "Luckily she has other charms. I can forgive her misguided notions about horses."

"Misguided notions indeed," Meera said under her breath. "Not just about horses."

"What's that?"

Meera half-sighed, half-chuckled. "She seems to have some misguided notions about Christopher as well," she clarified.

"That is for damn certain." Henry said with veracity. Meera raised her eyebrows. Henry's face softened slightly. "I admit I am not an impartial judge. Christopher is not my favorite person."

"Well, he's not my favorite person just now either." Meera agreed.

Henry grinned, but then his face got more serious. "For a long time, I could not see what Madison saw in him or why she continued to be his friend."

Meera was intrigued. "What changed your mind?" She asked.

"Who says I have?"

"You're here."

"Fair enough." Henry nodded. "I trust Madison unconditionally. If she sees something in Christopher then it must be there, no matter how deep."

Meera sighed wistfully. "What is it like, to have that kind of trust? That kind of love?"

Now it was Henry's turn to raise his eyebrows. He was silent for a few moments, trying to decide whether or not to speak. Eventually, he responded. "In the years since Madison and I married, Christopher has always been around. I wish I did not know him as well as I do, but thanks to Madison…" He shrugged his shoulders. "Anyways. In all that time, I have never seen him show anything beyond a physical fancy for a woman. He will dance with them and flirt with them. But he never forms any kind of attachment or allows anyone to get close to him. And yet he seems deeply concerned and troubled over you."

Meera resisted the urge to kick her mount into a gallop and run away from this conversation. Henry did not press her; he just smiled encouragingly and continued to ride alongside her.

"I am just so afraid." Meera finally said. Once she got those words out, it was like the floodgates opened. "I need him to trust me. I know I am hard-headed and impulsive, but I am also smart. I want him to believe in my judgment, to love me the way I am and not try to change me. I just do not want it to be so hard between us all the time." She had no idea why she was pouring her fears out to Henry, whom she barely knew. Maybe it was just easier to talk to someone who did not have all their own preconceptions and feelings about her.

In the distance, they could see clouds gathering on the horizon. Meera recognized the thick, dark hues that promised rain. A storm was coming.

Again, Henry was slow to respond and spoke carefully when he did. "I do not presume to know you or your mind. But perhaps what you are afraid are Christopher's attempts to constrain you, are really the actions of someone who holds you in the highest regard. Someone who loves you."

Meera felt her heart tighten at the word. *Love*. Yes, that word had been swirling around in her head for some time now. "But how do we start anew, after everything that has happened?" She said wistfully.

Henry chuckled. "If I had that answer, I would surely give it to you." He nodded towards the darkening sky. "I need to get back and check on Madison. Mornings are not always kind to her these days."

Warmed at the clear affection and love between her sister and her husband, Meera nodded and smiled. "Do go on. I will follow, but I fear I have overdone it a bit with my knee. Best I continue at a walk."

"Will you be alright?" Henry looked her over with concern, but Meera knew his heart was already back at the manor with Madison.

"Of course. If I am not back by midday, send a cart to lug me back." She said jokingly.

Henry laughed and saluted her as he urged his horse into a gallop and went ahead down the lane. Meera stared after him, turning over what he said in her mind. She thought she knew what love meant. She had been in love with Christopher before. But maybe now, as full-grown adults, love meant something different. Maybe it looked different.

It started to rain. As the drops started to hit her face, Meera felt that maybe there truly was a way forward for her and Christopher. The rain started to fall harder, a soft pattering in the grass and on the gravel of the road. Then there was a sharp, much louder sound. And everything went dark.

Chapter 21

When Meera's eyes opened, her immediate impulse was to shut them and hope she was having a terrible nightmare. She opened them again and found her surroundings unchanged. Her head hurt where she had been hit. She reached up to explore the extent of the damage. That was how she discovered her hands were tied. Panic started to rise in Meera's stomach and she actually felt bile begin to rise up her throat. No, no, no, no, no, she repeated to herself. She could not lose control and let fear take over. If she let that happen, her chances of survival would disappear. If she was going to make it out of this, back to Christopher, she needed to keep a clear head.

Christopher. Why had she been so stupid and stubborn? It had been a gunshot she heard. If she had just told him her suspicions, she would not be here now. She felt certain about that. Damn her pride.

Meera took another deep breath and tried to shut down that line of thinking as well. Neither fear nor regret was going to help her now. She looked around her; inside was dark but outside the daylight was still visible. She could hear the rain falling heavily. It appeared that she was tied up in a small cabin or shed. There wasn't any furniture aside from a chair and a stool. There was straw spread unevenly across the dark earth floor and a distinct animal smell. Meera was on the ground, tied to a metal anchor that was sunk into the dirt. She gave a tentative pull; the anchor felt secure but did wiggle a bit. That was a promising sign.

While she continued to move her wrists side to side, attempting to loosen the anchor from the earthen floor, she tried to assess her possibilities for escape. There were no windows. There was one door on the wall opposite to her. In the dim light she could not tell how it was secured, but it seemed a reasonable assumption that it was somehow locked from the outside. The building was in disrepair, and there were several areas where the wood of the walls looked rotted. If she could get her hands free, a strong throw of the stool or chair might create a hole in the wall.

There was a rustling at the door, someone fiddling with a lock, and then the door burst open. Meera recognized the red-haired man immediately from Paris. Up close, she could see that he was huge, dirty, and heavily muscled. His mouth had a cruel slant and the long scar running down his cheek made him look even more menacing. Meera felt the fear start to seep back in.

"Good. She's awake." The other man said. He was starkly different from the red-haired brute. He was neatly dressed, shorter, with tidy dark brown hair. He did not look like a brigand. Meera felt her courage start to return.

She lifted her chin defiantly. "I demand you release me at once."

The brown-haired man slapped her hard across the face.

Tears welled up in her eyes but Meera bit her lip to stop them from spilling out.

"You are not in charge, woman." He said coldly. He wiped his hand on his trousers as if sullied by touching her. Then he motioned the red-haired man forward. "Now, it is time to talk. How did you find out about the shipments?"

Meera tried to cross her arms, but of course could not because they were tied down. Instead she turned her head away and refused to look at either man. The red-haired man came forward and kicked her in the thigh. Meera cried out and involuntarily clutched her knee.

"How did you find out about the shipments?" Repeated the smaller man. He was clearly in charge, while the red-haired giant was the enforcer.

Meera closed her eyes, gripping her leg and trying to brace herself for the next blow.

The man sighed. "This does not have to be difficult. Let's focus on something more important." He spoke as if he were conducting a cordial business transaction. But Meera could still feel the sting on her cheek where he had struck her. She kept one eye on him and the other on his henchman "Who else knows about the orders?"

"No one." Meera said immediately.

The man actually laughed. It was a cruel, humorless sound. "We already know about your

English lord. He went to all the trouble to bring you here from Paris. He is our next stop."

She couldn't think straight; all she could feel was fear. "He does not know anything." She said desperately.

"Your kind always think the lower-class are stupid." He motioned the enforcer forward, and the red-haired man pushed down hard on her knee.

Tears started to stream down Meera's cheeks. The pain was unbearable. "He doesn't know anything about this," she sobbed. "I have just been using him. I've taken him to my bed. A man will do anything for a woman if she gives him what he wants in the bedroom."

He paused to consider what she had said, looking at her closely. "I suppose you would be quite a compelling tumble," he acknowledged, raking his eyes over her body. The red-haired man made a sound of appreciation that shook Meera more than anything else thus far.

Meera tried to seize on his attention, hoping to distract him from Christopher. "I overheard about the textile orders at a party in Paris. I wanted to know what was going on. But I haven't found anything out. Just the names of a few warehouses and companies. That's it. I am just a woman. No one tells me anything." She insisted. It was ironic, she thought fleetingly, that the very things that so deeply frustrated her she now hoped would be able to save her.

"You could be telling the truth," the man conceded. "But you could also be lying." The red-haired man stepped forward again, but the other held up his hand to stop him. "We need to speak with the Earl."

The huge, burly man looked disappointed. He gave her a half-hearted kick as he walked past her to the door. The other man paused for a moment and looked as if he might say more to her, but then shook his head dismissively and left without a backward glance. As they left, she heard the distinctive metal jangle of a lock and a heavy thud that she could only assume was some way of barring the door.

Alone again, Meera felt the tears begin to flow freely. Her knee ached from abuse and she could feel her lip swelling where he had slapped her. But mostly she cried for herself and for Christopher. This whole mess was her fault. She never dreamed it would get this far. When the initial burst of emotion subsided, Meera realized that it was getting later in the day. The light coming through the cracks of the shoddy building were more muted. Back at Shipford Hall, it would soon be time to dress for the evening meal.

Meera had a startling realization. They might not even know she was missing. Henry would have returned and gone straight to Madison. She and Christopher had been studiously avoiding each other for days. They would only realize her absence when she failed to appear for supper. She had no idea where she had been taken; it might take them days to find her. She was well and truly alone.

The fear started to recede and adrenaline took its place. She had to get out of here on her own. The only reason she was left alone now was because her captors assumed she was a powerless woman. Meera gave another tug on the anchor holding her tied hands in place. It moved slightly. She pulled harder and was rewarded by a little shifting in the dirt. She felt a glimmer of hope. She could do this.

Chapter 22

Christopher thought about Madison's words all day. He was in love with Meera. He envisioned a hundred scenarios for how their relationship could unfold. But in every imagined version of his life, she was in it. The fear was still there: the fear she would leave again; the fear he would not be enough to hold her. But if he did not tell her how he felt and ask her to stay then he would regret it.

He waited restlessly for his valet to finish straightening his evening attire. If he could just get through this meal, then he would be able to find somewhere quiet to talk to Meera alone. Christopher felt himself tighten with desire and anticipation just at the thought of being alone with her. It seemed like weeks rather than days since they made love in the bed he stood beside at that very moment. *God, he needed her.* Heart, body, and soul.

Maybe he would try and talk to her before supper, Christopher thought as he thanked his valet and headed downstairs. They would probably be late to the meal and it would be anything but polite to Madison and Henry. But Madison would understand, Christopher thought to himself with a smile.

"Good evening," Christopher said as he entered, finding Madison and Henry already assembled.

Madison immediately took note of his flushed, eager demeanor and felt a surge of hopefulness. Henry had recounted his morning conversation with Meera, and Madison was beginning to think that perhaps her sister and erstwhile friend would sort things out after all. "You're looking well," she observed.

"Not as well as you," Christopher said. "You must have stolen a nap, while I have been awake since dawn with no respite."

Madison shrugged. "Naps are a woman's prerogative when she is with child."

"I will defer to you on that."

"I would defer to her on everything at this point, she's getting to be bloody demanding." Henry said as he joined them.

Madison swatted his arm. "You should have taken a nap as well. Waking up at dawn and spending hours in the saddle would put me in a sour mood too."

"I had quite a pleasant morning with Meera." Henry said. "Your sister is a fine equestrian."

Madison rolled her eyes. "All of you and your obsession with horses, I will never understand." She said dismissively. "We did spend a lovely afternoon exploring your gardens, Christopher. You have curated quite an attractive residence here. Shame on you for not inviting us sooner."

"I did not exactly invite you this time," Christopher pointed out with a wry smile.

"I could not very well stay away once I found out my sister was here," Madison reasoned.

"Where is Meera? It must be nearly time to go through." Christopher looked towards the door expectantly, but the footman stood there alone.

"We haven't seen her this afternoon. I assumed maybe you two were making amends?" Madison said, one eyebrow raised suggestively.

Christopher frowned. "No, I have not seen her at all today." Had she returned to hiding in her room refusing to talk to him? That did not bode well for the conversation he hoped to have this evening.

"We went out riding this morning. I came back to check on Madison; Meera said she wanted to stay out a bit longer. She said she would be returning shortly behind me…that was at midday." Henry said.

Christopher was starting to get an uneasy feeling in his stomach. The butler entered from the dining room to announce the meal was ready to be served, but Christopher cut him off. "Rhodes, did you see Miss Hutton when she returned from her morning ride?"

"No, my lord. I have not seen her since she left early this morning."

A disturbing thought began to form in Christopher's mind. "Did anyone see her return?"

Rhodes wrinkled his brow. "I do not know, sir." The look on Christopher's face spoke as clearly as words. "I will go and find out immediately, my lord." Rhodes said, turning on his heel.

"You check with the household staff. I will go down to the stables." Christopher said as he followed the butler out of the door. He heard Henry behind him, following his urgent steps.

They reached the stables quickly. "Where is Mr. Arnold?" He demanded of the first groom he saw. He heard the gruffness of his voice but did not have time to care.

"He had the afternoon off, my lord." The young man said.

"Did you see Miss Hutton return?"

The groom looked confused. "I just came on this morning, sir. I do not know Miss Hutton."

"*Christ*," Christopher swore. He brushed past the groom and into the stables. As his long strides took him down the aisle of stalls, he felt his panic rising. He rounded the corner, where just two stalls stood by themselves. Olympias' stall was empty.

Henry caught up with him a heartbeat later.

"Her horse isn't here." Christopher said.

"Could she be in the pasture?" Henry asked.

Christopher shook his head. "It was empty when we walked by."

Neither of them wasted a second. They were back at the house in minutes, where Madison was wringing her hands. The housekeeper, Mrs. Adams, arrived just ahead of them. "None of the maids have seen Miss Hutton since she departed this morning. I checked her room myself. And your rooms as well, my lord," the woman glanced downward, clearly embarrassed. "She is not there."

Rhodes entered the room just in time to hear Mrs. Adams' words. "The kitchen staff and footmen have not seen her either, my lord." He reported

"She's been taken." Christopher said.

"You cannot possibly know that, Christopher." Madison said, her eyes filling with tears. "She could have taken another fall from her horse, and be slow making her way home. It happened before."

"This is not an accident or a coincidence. I need to go to Southampton straightaway. I must speak with John Purdue. Have my horse saddled." He directed Rhodes, who immediately disappeared. Christopher turned back to Madison and Henry. "John said they had suspects. He is my best chance of finding her. I will send word as soon as I can."

"I will go with you." Henry said. He clearly thought Christopher was going to argue. But Christopher was far past the point of petty dislike.

"Fine. I have no idea what we will be walking into."

"There is no one here." Christopher kicked the wall in frustration. They had been to three of the places on the list of that John had provided them. All were storage locations associated with the two textile companies that the authorities were still covertly investigating. All were deserted except for shipping crates and filth.

"We have two more to check. If we move quickly, we might be able to reach the next before dawn." Henry said, looking at the dark sky and trying to judge the time.

Christopher gritted his teeth and climbed back aboard his horse. First he had felt disbelief, then rage, and then determination. But as possibilities for finding Meera started to fall away, he started to feel fear.

"We will find her." Henry said, mounting up beside Christopher.

"You don't know that."

"We will."

"*Damnit, will you just be quiet?* We don't know anything! She could be anywhere! She could be dead!" Christopher yelled. He felt his horse shift uneasily under him.

"We will find her." Henry repeated calmly.

"What makes you so damn sure?"

"Because you love her. And when you love someone, you never stop searching." Henry said simply.

Christopher swore under his breath. "Let's go." He said, kicking his horse into a run.

Chapter 23

As they slowly approached the little ramshackle building it became obvious that it was occupied. Whatever lantern was inside was dim; not a lot of light was coming through the cracks and holes of rotted wood. But the occupants were making no effort to keep their voices quiet and they were clearly arguing. It looked like a small stable that had long been abandoned for newer facilities. The farm itself was not remote; in fact, it was quite close to Southampton by the sea road. But this little building was on a forgotten corner of the large farm, and well hidden by a copse of trees. Christopher could see its appeal to a smuggler.

"How many do you think there are?" Henry whispered. They left their horses tied a hundred yards back and approached on foot. They were crouched about ten yards from the building.

"Two who have spoken. Can you make out what they are saying?"

Henry shook his head. The fact that Christopher could see him do it in the rising light meant that dawn was upon them. They would not have the cover of darkness for long.

"The door could be barred from the inside. But it doesn't look like it would take much to knock it down." Henry observed.

"I doubt its locked. Whoever these two are, they do not seem concerned about being disturbed." Christopher said. He squinted to see more in the fading darkness. No windows, but a sizeable hole of rotted away wood on the wall adjacent to the door. "You try the door first. Hit it with as much force as you can. If it doesn't give right away, I will kick in the wall at the side there."

Henry nodded and silently pulled out the pistol he had tucked into his belt, checking the powder. Christopher did the same. He also reached down and loosened the knife that he kept in his boot. "Ready?" Christopher asked. Henry nodded.

The voices got clearer as they approached but neither man paused to listen. Henry hit the door hard and it gave way instantly with a loud crash. Christopher ran in behind him and barely dodged the flying stool aimed at his head. Henry was engaged in fisticuffs with a huge red-haired man. The huge red-haired man from Paris, Christopher realized immediately. Before he could form the next thought, the other man ran at him. Christopher dodged to the side, and the smaller man hit the wall behind him. The entire building gave a loud groan. He hit the other man hard in the face and brought his knee up with force between his legs. The man fell to his knees, and Christopher hit his dark-haired head with the heavy butt of his pistol. He fell to the ground unconscious.

Henry was doing admirably against his opponent, but the brutish man was considerably taller and bulkier. Henry was doing his best just to make sure he himself did not get pummeled. Christopher looked around the room. He grabbed an overturned chair from the corner and brought it down on the back of the man's head. It did not knock him out, but he stumbled and it gave them the opening they needed. When he regained his balance, he was looking at the drawn barrels of both Christopher and Henry's pistols.

"Tie him up." Christopher nodded to the unconscious man. The red-haired man frowned but did as he was told. When Christopher instructed him to turn around and place his hands behind his back so that Henry could tie them, he looked for a second like he was considering trying something. But the look of cold determination on Christopher's face must have dissuaded him.

He was right to be leery. Christopher had no doubt they had found the right place. But Meera was not here. And Christopher was on a knife's edge.

The smaller, dark-haired man was coming around. He jerked into consciousness and pulled instinctively on the restraints. He looked around wildly, and then his eyes landed on Henry and Christopher. He stilled.

"Where is she?" Christopher said bluntly.

Neither man spoke. Henry raised his eyebrows and shook his head. "Your mistake." He said quietly.

Christopher did not hesitate. He kicked each man hard in the stomach. The big man tried to fight back and Christopher kicked him again. He was not even thinking. He had never been in a serious fight; just the brawls of adolescence and an occasional round in the boxing ring. He was not a violent man. But he was completely taken over by rage and fear.

"Where is she?" Christopher repeated. Neither man responded and he started to advance again. Henry held up a hand to stop him.

"Now, perhaps they need a little persuasion." Henry said. Christopher looked murderous. Henry ignored him and turned back to the two men. "Let's be logical here. We have you in our power. The constable and his staff know where we are and our purpose in coming here. There is no possibility of escape."

Henry paused dramatically and Christopher felt his frustration rise. They did not have time for this. What if Meera was hurt? What if she needed them *now*?

"We can make a case to the authorities. Tell them you helped us. Tell them to be lenient." Henry said quickly, sensing Christopher's tenuousness.

The smaller man scoffed. "As if you would."

Henry sighed. "Well, I tried." He turned his back as Christopher advanced on them. There was the crunch of flesh, followed by groans of pain.

"Where is she?" Christopher repeated a third time.

"Not here." The first man said, spitting blood out of his mouth.

"Not anymore." The big man said under his breath. His companion elbowed him hard for this.

Christopher's head whipped around. "She was here." He looked wildly around the little cabin for some sign of Meera but found none.

"Where did you take her?" Henry said.

"Who said we took her anywhere?" The smaller man said defiantly.

"Are you saying she escaped?" Christopher pressed.

"I am not saying that. All I am saying is that she is not here."

"Then where is she? With your employer? Who do you work for?" Christopher grabbed the small man by his shirt front and shook him hard.

"I work for myself." The man said through gritted teeth.

"The hell you do."

Christopher did not realize what was happening until he felt the considerable weight of the other man slump against him. He jumped back, and saw the knife clatter to the ground. The red-haired beast must have had it on his person. He managed to get it out and cut his ties. He seized the opportunity when Christopher got close to try and take him down. But Henry beat him to it.

A trickle of blood ran from behind his ear where Henry had hit him. Henry leaned down and checked his pulse.

"He's not dead." Henry said, wiping his hand on his breeches.

Christopher looked from the huge slumped form and back to Henry, who stood there calm as ever. "Thank you." He said simply.

Henry nodded. He held Christopher's gaze for a moment, and then turned back to the remaining villain. "The scheme is up. We have alerted the authorities, and once you are brought in your entire enterprise will be unraveled. You have nothing left to gain except by helping us. Where is she?"

The man smiled malevolently. "I do not know where she is. Only God almighty knows that now."

Without hesitation, Henry knocked him unconscious as well.

Christopher did not pause. He left the building wordlessly. Henry took a minute to secure the two men and then followed Christopher out. Christopher covered the ground quickly and was already mounted on his horse.

"Where are you going? We need to get these two to the authorities."

"You heard him. She could be dead."

"He just said it to rile you."

"But she could be dead."

"Christopher, I know you are afraid, but think about this logically. What reason would they have to kill her?" Henry said, catching the reins of Christopher's horse to prevent him from riding away.

Christopher saw red. "Of course I am afraid! I just got her back, and now she is taken away from me because I could not keep her safe!" He yelled. He yanked his reins free. "I have to find her, and I have to find her now."

"What do you want me to do with those two?" Henry motioned back to the cabin.

"Get rid of them. Take them to the authorities. Make them disappear. I don't care."

Chapter 24

Meera made it to the outskirts of Southampton as dawn was breaking. There were very few people about. She did not want to draw attention to herself, so she took shelter by a small pond twenty yards or so off the road. The grass was soft and there were a few trees which hid her from sight and provided cover. She was desperately tired and her knee ached. She had hobbled along half the night. Originally, she tried to make her way through the brush and grass along the roadside, where she could more easily stay out of sight in case she was pursued. But her knee could not handle the rough terrain and before long she gave in and walked up on the road itself.

After several hours of pulling at her restraint, Meera was able to work her hands free. The door was bolted from the outside, but a few hard kicks from her uninjured leg and the rotted out lower section of wall gave way. Crouching low on her hands and knees, she was able to crawl out of the little shack. Then she walked. A long slog in the dark with nothing to do but think. She was physically and mentally exhausted.

She nearly collapsed onto the ground, thankful to lean back against a tree trunk and finally rest. She intended to close her eyes and sleep until the afternoon. By then the city would be bustling and she would be able to carry out her business unnoticed. But as soon as she closed her eyes, she saw Christopher.

Her whole body ached, but when she thought of Christopher all of that was eclipsed by the pain in her heart. She loved him. She loved the boy he had been, the man he had become, and the life they had started to build together. Whatever their differences were, and there were many, she had become certain that they could figure them out. It all seemed so petty and trivial in face of the life and death scenarios of the last twelve hours. But they would never know. They would never get the chance.

She cried herself to sleep.

When she awoke, the sun was high in the sky. Meera pulled herself to her feet, smoothed her dress and tidied herself using the clear water from the pond as best she could. Then she set off into Southampton. She had never been there before, but it did not take much asking to locate a banking house. There, she was able to draw the money she needed. She had no money on her when she was taken, but she did have the jewelry she was wearing. She exchanged her earrings, necklace, and two rings for money. It was not a lot, but if she was careful it would be enough to get her by until she could get settled and send for more.

She had to leave England. If Christopher had been telling her the truth, and at this point she had to believe that he was, then they were no closer to solving this mystery than when they had arrived in England. Worse, the villains knew who she was and where she could be found. If she went back to Shipford Hall, back to Christopher, it would only be a matter of time before they tried again. And this time they might try to get to Christopher instead. She could not let that happen. If she left, then maybe it would go away. And Christopher would be safe.

An hour later, she had successfully booked passage on a ship bound for Spain. Meera had a few acquaintances there whom she met while in Paris. She felt confident they would give her shelter as she got her feet under her. The man who sold her the ticket looked at her suspiciously, especially when she said she had no luggage. Meera looked down at her crumpled gown and cloak. She did not have much money left, but perhaps it would be worth looking into a simple muslin frock that was at least clean.

Busy frowning down at her attire and not watching where she was going, Meera ran straight into someone's back. "Pardon me, I am so sorry!" She said automatically, looking up in embarrassment. Her eyes widened and for a moment she thought she was imagining things. "Christopher!" She cried, and then collapsed into his arms.

Christopher thought at first that he must be dreaming. In the past twenty-four hours he had not slept and had hardly eaten or drank anything. But as his arms went instinctively around her, he felt her warmth against his body. He felt her heaving sobs on his chest and the wetness of her tears on the front of his shirt. "Meera." He barely dared to say her name for fear she would disappear. He put his hand underneath her chin and pulled her face up to his. "Are you alright? Are you hurt?" He managed to say, his voice sounding strangled.

"No, no, I am fine." Meera assured him. She touched the side of his face and then stood on her toes to reach her lips up to his. They kissed ardently. Christopher lifted her off the ground and held her so tightly to him that it almost hurt. But Meera did not care.

When they broke apart to breathe, Christopher cupped her face to keep her close. They stood there for a few moments, foreheads pressed together as the emotions washed over them like waves. "I thought I lost you." Christopher said.

Meera felt her heart start to break. It took all of her strength to pull herself back, but she was not able to keep the pain off her of her face. Christopher's eyes widened in alarm. "What is it? What is wrong?" He looked around them, instinctively searching for some outward cause of disquiet. His eyes landed on the placard above the door she had exited.

Christopher felt like he had been punched in the gut. His mouth could barely form the words. "Are you leaving?"

He could see the answer in her face before she even opened her mouth to respond

He turned away, ripping his hands out of hers and turning his back to her. He closed his eyes as the ripples of pain coursed through him. But then just as quickly as he pulled away, Christopher turned back. He took Meera's hands in his, stroking them tenderly. He looked into her big, dark, beautiful, confused eyes and somehow found the courage to speak. "Meera, I know that things have been hard between us. I recognize now it was my fault as much as yours. But I know what is important now. Whatever freedoms you want: travel, independence, anything; I won't try to stop you. But I cannot lose you again." He leaned down and kissed her, at first passionately as he tried to pour all of his desire into the kiss. And then softer, with utter tenderness. "I love you, Meera. Not as a naïve boy loved a headstrong girl. But as a man, who knows myself, a man who loves you and the woman you are now."

Meera felt her heart flutter and then lurch in her chest. She supposed she had known it for some time now: that the love between them had never really died. That it laid dormant, waiting, until fate brought them together again to be rekindled brighter and stronger than ever. Well, fate be damned. She would not allow fate to take him from her.

Maybe she would not have him herself, to have and to hold. But she would know he was alive, safe. And she could love him from afar, knowing that. What she could not bear was the thought of living in a world without him in it. She would never forgive herself is she stayed and something happened to him.

For what seemed the hundredth time in the last two days, tears were falling down her cheeks. Meera did not even try to stop them. Christopher held her hands tightly, staring into her eyes and imploring a response. She wanted to fall back into his arms and tell him how much she loved him. But she didn't.

"I am sorry, Christopher. So very sorry." Meera pulled her hands free and backed away. "I have to go," she said. She saw the disbelief in Christopher's eyes, but knew that if she stayed a moment longer she would lose her resolve. Without another word she turned and hurried away down the street, her chest heaving with sobs she could no longer contain.

Chapter 25

He did not know why he did it. At first, he could not move at all. He watched Meera walk away down the street, making her way to the nearby dockside and towards a large multi-mast ship. For some unknown reason, Christopher followed. He had no intention of trying to convince her to change her mind. She had spoken clearly and with conviction.

Now he was standing on the dock staring at the ship as the crew prepared to sail. He felt totally numb. Maybe there was just a limit to how much emotion one person could feel in a given amount of time and the last day had exhausted everything he had. Christopher laid his entire heart out before Meera and she chose to walk away. So, he stood there wordlessly watching as ropes were thrown and last pieces of cargo hoisted aboard. He would stay until the ship lifted anchor, and Meera was truly gone from his life.

Meera cried until her chest hurt. Her eyes were raw and puffy, but there was no one to see and even if there had been she would not have cared. She was in a tiny cabin aboard ship waiting for the evening tide. *This is wrong, it's all wrong,* she kept thinking over and over again. Right now, she was not the strong, independent woman she prided herself on being. She was a wreck, and she knew it.

She sat up in her narrow bunk and looked around the room. There was maybe two feet of floor space that ran alongside the bunk. In her urgency to get away from Christopher, she forgot about the possibility of acquiring a dress or any kind of creature comforts. So the room was totally barren: four walls, a bed, and her. She had never felt so alone in her life.

Suddenly, the walls of the cabin seemed to be closing in on her. Overwhelmed by her emotions and the claustrophobic little room, she fled desperately out onto the deck.

The cold sea air would normally have chilled her but in that moment, it was a comfort. Closing her eyes, Meera gulped down breaths of the salty air and slowly started to get a handle on herself. She gripped the railing at the edge of the ship and tried to find her inner strength. When she finally opened her eyes, she was struck by how the world around her was just moving along like normal. The crewmen were readying the ship; passengers, merchants, and seamen crowded the quay below. She watched them with envy; their lives had not just been torn apart.

She saw Christopher. He was standing about halfway down the dock, looking up at the ship. Meera did not think he saw her; his eyes may be trained on the ship but his mind was clearly elsewhere. She took a few steps back from the railing, so that she could still see him but was not as easily visible from the dock. It seemed like torture to stand there in plain sight while she sailed away from him.

"Excuse me, you are Miss Hutton, correct?" A tall, well-dressed gentleman asked as he approached her.

Meera nodded and smiled automatically, unconsciously letting years of society experience take over. "Yes, I am Meera Hutton."

"I am Captain Walsh," the man said. Meera was not surprised; his attire clearly marked him out as more than the average seaman. "I am sorry to tell you, Miss Hutton, but our departure has been delayed."

"Delayed?" Meera echoed.

"Yes, Miss. A few hours at least, possibly until tomorrow."

"I see." Meera frowned. She was not afraid she would lose her resolve, only that the longer she stayed within reach of Christopher the longer the pain of separation would be drawn out. But then, maybe it did not matter. She doubted the pain of losing Christopher would ever fade away.

"It is completely out of my control, I am sorry to say. The authorities have apprehended a high-profile criminal and several of his associates, and they are not letting any ships leave port for the time being." The captain explained.

Meera felt a little flicker somewhere deep inside of her, but she did not dare to acknowledge it. "A criminal, you say. What crime could possibly justify closing the port?" She asked, her voice thick.

"Smugglers. Apparently, there is an international component, something out of France. Unfortunately, we do get a fair number of French ships here in Southampton." Captain Walsh answered. He kept glancing over Meera's shoulder, clearly eager to end the conversation. He had done his duty and alerted the passenger, and now he had other things to get to. "If you will excuse me, Miss Hutton, I—"

Meera put her hand on his arm to stop him from leaving. "Please, Captain, I am sorry to detain you. Do you know anything else about this matter? Anything at all?"

Captain Walsh frowned, clearly confused at her earnestness. "There were two men brought in this morning, by a lord of some kind. He turned them over to the authorities. They have arrested the Earl of Rockwood. It is going to be quite a scandal."

Meera felt the ember of hope in her chest kindle into a flame. Her tormenters had been caught. The earl they had spoken of, the man in charge, had been arrested. It was over.

Taking her moment of silence to extricate himself, the captain continued down the deck. Waves of relief washed over Meera. She rushed to the ship's railing, her eyes going straight to Christopher. But he was not there.

Frantically, she searched up and down the quay. She spotted him walking away from the ship towards the street. "Christopher!" She yelled, leaning precipitously far over the railing. "Christopher!" She bellowed again, but to no avail. There was too much noise on the busy docks.

She ran frantically towards the captain, who had stopped mid-conversation with a crewman and was watching Meera with astonishment. "Please, Captain Walsh, I need to get off the ship immediately."

"I can have a gangway lowered down, Miss Hutton, but it will take a few minutes." Captain Walsh answered.

"I don't have a few minutes. He will be gone!" Meera said frantically. She turned back and searched through the crowd, locating Christopher again. She turned to a nearby crewman. "Can you swing me down on a rope?"

The man was shocked. Overhearing her, Captain Walsh actually laughed out loud.

"Can you swing me down on a rope?" Meera repeated urgently.

"Begging your pardon, ma'am, but it's not exactly proper…" the young sailor said, looking at her dubiously.

Meera almost growled in frustration, but then she remembered something. She reached into the deep inner pocket of her cloak and fished out one of the banknotes stowed there. She pressed it into his hand. "Please, get me down to the dock."

The crewman looked at his captain, who put up his hands in surrender. With a shrug, the young man led Meera over to a rope secured for that purpose, put one arm firmly around her waist, and swung her down to the dock. They landed with a thud and Meera lost her balance, stumbling to her knees. In her state of euphoria, she did not even process the jolt of pain to her already injured knee. People were staring at the commotion. But Meera was completely oblivious as she gained her feet and started running through the crowd.

Christopher turned around, becoming aware of the unfolding stir, and watched in disbelief as Meera extricated herself from the sailor and his rope and started towards him. When she finally got to him, she reached for his hands, but he pulled them away and stepped back from her automatically.

Meera bit her lip and forced herself to take a deep breath. She could not blame him for being wary of her. "Christopher, I am so sorry. Please, please, do not go. All I wanted was to protect you. I was so afraid…" Meera felt her lips trembling. She thought she had exhausted her supply of tears, but somehow, they started to fall again. "I was so afraid they were going to come after you. I had to go. I didn't want to. Lord, it was the last thing I wanted to do. All I want is to be with you. I love you! But I had to go. I could not stay and risk them hurting you. I love you so much. I just couldn't bear to have anything happen to you. I just love you—"

"Shhhh," Christopher said, pulling her into his arms. She was quickly becoming unintelligible, but Christopher wasn't listening anymore. He was kissing her cheeks, her forehead, her lips; he kissed away the tears.

"I love you." Meera managed to say with a heave of her chest.

Christopher cupped her chin, tenderly touching the edge of her face. "I love you too," he said. "But swinging down from ships on a rope is exactly the kind of dangerous nonsense I would rather you did not do."

Meera laughed through her tears, which were finally slowing. "Remember, you promised me whatever freedoms I needed." She said jokingly.

"So I did," Christopher said with a smile. Then he pulled her against him, crushing her close. "As long as you always come right back here to me, you can have whatever you want."

Epilogue

The sun was starting its descent. It cast long rays of gold, amber, and rose over the rolling hills beyond Shipford Hall. It was well past time to go inside and dress for the evening meal, but neither of the figures sitting on the woven wicker chaise moved. Their fingers were twined together, and her head lay peacefully on his shoulder.

"I think we should get married here." Meera said as she gazed out at the lovely scene. For the first time in her life she felt a complete sense of peace and belonging.

Christopher glanced down at her. "Not in a church? Not in Paris?" He said, surprised.

"You think a church would have us?" Meera laughed out loud and then shook her head, speaking more seriously: "No, here. Outside with the trees and the house in the background. It is just the most perfect place I have ever been."

"You won't get an argument from me." Christopher stroked her head where it rested on his shoulder.

"We'll have to wait until Madison has the baby. I hope the weather doesn't turn on us, that will be past the best part of summer." She mused, tracing her finger along the long line of his thigh.

"We could wait until the spring," Christopher suggested. Meera sat up instantly in surprise, narrowing her eyes as she caught sight of his smirking face. She jabbed him playfully in the ribs and then set her chin on his shoulder so her face was only a couple of inches from his.

"Now that my mother knows about us, I think the sooner the better. I do not think she will be able to handle us living in sin much longer. Besides," she added, "I don't want to wait an entire year to go to Africa."

"Africa?"

"Yes, I was thinking Africa for our honeymoon."

"Of course you were."

Meera was about to answer that with a kiss when she heard footfalls behind them. She looked over Christopher's shoulder to see Rhodes, the butler, and another man she did not recognize approaching.

"My lord, I beg your pardon," Rhodes bowed. "Sir Richard Burbank, the constable from Southampton, asked to see you. I know it is later than you usually accept callers, but given everything that has happened…"

"Of course," Christopher started to get to his feet but the other man stepped forward.

"Please, Lord Bowden, I do not wish to intrude." Sir Richard said quickly. Christopher stood anyways, shaking the man's hand, and motioned him to sit across from them. When he sat back down, he immediately curled his arm around Meera's shoulders. She reached for his hand and held it tightly in hers.

"I wanted to come here and speak to you personally, Lord Bowden. The information you passed along to Mr. Purdue, the documentation you secured through your contacts in London, the connection back to Paris – all of it was essential to the capture and disruption of the smuggling chain. Without your help, I do not think the arrests would have been possible; to be able to connect it all back to the Earl of Rockwood…it really is something." Sir Richard explained. "I wanted to thank you, humbly, for helping solve this matter and bring these villains to justice."

Christopher nodded slowly, turning his eyes away from the constable. "You are welcome, of course. But I must give credit where credit is due, Sir Richard. My fiancée, Miss Hutton, is really responsible for uncovering this matter." Both men turned to Meera, who was momentarily surprised.

Sir Richard raised his eyebrows. "I see…" he said, though it was clear he did not really comprehend at all.

"Miss Hutton was the one who realized something untoward was going on in Paris, narrowing down the trade and some of the victims. It was only at her insistence that I became involved. Her determination to see justice served is the only reason we are here at all today." Christopher continued, his voice clear and articulate. Meera felt like she was glowing. Things really were different between them now. The fear of who they used to be was finally gone.

For his part, Sir Richard took it all in stride. "Well, then I extend my thanks to you directly, Miss Hutton." He said, bowing to her. Meera smiled graciously.

"If I may, Sir Richard, I do have one question?" She asked.

"Anything, my lady."

"What were they smuggling?"

Sir Richard smiled grimly. "Artifacts. Antiques. Treasures. Mostly out of Africa; some from Asia. They would use large textile shipments to secret away the valuables. Because the noblesse is not known for their attention to detail, they were an ideal target. No one noticed the small discrepancies in receipts – add a crate here, a bolt of fabric there – to a large order and instead slip in something else."

"I certainly would not notice if someone snuck something secret amongst the mountains of your trunks that keep arriving from Paris." Christopher said sardonically. Meera elbowed him again in the ribs, more covertly this time.

"Thank you for coming, Sir Richard," she said sweetly. The constable bowed to them both and then disappeared along the path back up to the house.

"So…Africa?" Meera said casually, turning her face back to Christopher.

"Anywhere, my love. As long as I have you." He pulled her close, and kissed her.

If you enjoyed *Love Once Lost*…

Please leave a positive review on Amazon or Goodreads

Reviews are essential for independent authors! As an emerging author, I read every review you write and take it to heart as I dream up new romances. Your review really does make an impact. It helps other readers find and enjoy these characters and their stories. Thank you for your time. -Cara

Read the rest of the Hesitant Husbands Series:

Meant to be Mine: A Regency Romance

A Love Match for the Marquess

Visit caramaxwellromance.com for previews of upcoming books and special offers. Follow @caramaxwellromance on Instagram for updates and exclusive content.

About the Author

Bringing fresh perspective and punch to the genre readers already know and love, Cara Maxwell is dedicated to writing spirited heroines and irresistible rogues who you will root for every time. A lifetime reader of romance, Cara put pen to paper (or rather, fingers to keyboard) in 2019 and published her first book. She hasn't slowed down from there.

Cara is an avid traveler. As she explores new places, she imagines her characters walking hand-in-hand down a cobblestone path or sharing a passionate kiss in a secluded alcove. Cara is living out her own happily ever after in Seattle, Washington, where she resides with her husband, daughter, and two cats, RoseArt and Etch-a-Sketch.

Printed in Great Britain
by Amazon